M000098627

MASON'S GRAY

MASON'S GRAY

Geri' Myers Goodwin

JONES MEDIA
PUBLISHING

Mason's Gray Copyright © 2018 by Geri' Myers Goodwin.

All rights reserved. No part of this publication may be reproduced, distributed, or transmitted in any form or by any means, including photocopying, recording, or other electronic or mechanical methods, without the prior written permission of the author, except in the case of brief quotations embodied in critical reviews and certain other noncommercial uses permitted by copyright law.

Jones Media Publishing
10645 N. Tatum Blvd. Ste. 200-166
Phoenix, AZ 85028
www.JonesMediaPublishing.com

Printed in the United States of America.

ISBN-13: 978-1-945849-59-6

DEDICATION

In Loving Memory of Glenda Ann Beck

CONTENTS

CHAPTER ONE

TREASURED PAST, NEW BEGINNINGS

Morgan Gray pushed the last of what she could fit into the back of her white SUV, tucking and shoving to get the door to go down.

"Come on! Get in there!" she said, finally slamming the door shut. Dust filtered in the air, causing her to cough and step back.

Waving the haze away with her hands, she walked down to the edge of the driveway. Kneeling, she ran her fingers over the handprints her three children had stamped into the concrete so many years ago. Tears began to stream down her face as she remembered Justin playing basketball every night until the sun went down. Her eyes drifted to look at the weathered hoop still hanging over the garage door, the tattered and torn netting barely hanging on.

Glancing down the street, she had a phantom vision of Ashley pulling Brooklyn in a red wagon on the sidewalk, waving at neighbors and stopping to rescue every stray animal they came across. Swiping the tears before they dropped, Morgan shook her head and grinned at the memory. She'd nearly pulled every hair out of her head from the numerous times the girls walked into the house clutching a scraggly animal in their arms, staring at her with pleading eyes.

Slowly she stood, shoving her hands into the back pockets of her blue jeans. The creaking sound of the "For Sale" sign swinging back and forth from the light breeze captured her attention. The word *SOLD* in big bold letters jumped out at her, reminding Morgan it was time to leave.

"This is really happening," she whispered.

Climbing into the SUV, Morgan squeezed the steering wheel tight and lay her head down. As the engine purred, her wrists twisted and turned in an effort to let go.

Since the loss of her soul mate only eight years prior, she'd overcome so much. At the young age of forty, Morgan had become not only a widow, but a single parent as well. She'd worked desperately to juggle bills and maintain a normal routine for the kids. Inevitably, the empty-nest syndrome Morgan had dreaded became a reality. Brooklyn had moved to Venice Beach as soon as the diploma hit her hand. Justin and Ashley lived in Denver now, sharing a house and surprisingly managing to get along.

Morgan tilted her head to gaze at the passenger seat where her brand new digital camera sat. Her next journey was at her fingertips.

"Why am I so damn scared? I'm such a coward," she said out loud.

She lifted her head in a rush and determination flooded her veins.

Enough, Morgan! Put your big-girl pants on and get the fuck out of here!

Her right foot revved the engine as her hand came down to the console to shift into reverse. Her brown ponytail swung, bouncing in reaction to the SUV peeling out of the driveway. She reached over to turn up the radio before throwing the SUV into drive, cranking the volume so high the bass throbbed. Her upper body jerked forward as she shifted gears and set off down the street. It only took a second for Morgan to glance up and look out the rearview mirror. She admired the sunrise glowing behind her.

"I will miss you, Arizona," she whispered.

Feeling as though she were running from her past, she focused on the headlights sparkling off the asphalt, directing her toward the future that awaited her. Suddenly, the car seemed to move effortlessly as if it were driving itself.

"Santa Cruz … here I come."

* * *

Fighting fatigue along the way, she drove determinedly to reach Santa Cruz before nightfall, stopping only for pee breaks and gas. Her brown eyes, feeling blurry, had begun to play tricks on her. She couldn't remember what she'd seen in the last forty miles or so and knew it wasn't safe to be behind the wheel much longer.

Rolling down the window to let in some fresh air, Morgan shifted in her seat and began massaging the back of her aching neck. As she took in a whiff of the sea breeze, her eyes became more alert. Fatigue turned to excitement. She'd finally made it.

Before long, the GPS had her pulling into the driveway of the beachfront cottage that would be her home for the summer season. Turning off the engine, she blew out a long slow breath. She sat in the SUV and stared at the cottage in awe. It was a vision of paradise with pink bougainvillea climbing the white stucco walls and hibiscus plants in blue ceramic pots on each side of the front door.

Her hand fumbled to open the car door as the anticipation to go inside surfaced. One foot swung out the car door, landing on a cobblestone driveway.

"Whoa—nice," she said admiring each imperfect stone. Extracting the key from the lockbox on the porch, she entered the one-bedroom cottage. Sucking in a quick breath, she choked on her own words.

"This is … this is incredible."

She took off for the sliding-glass door that led to the back deck. She grabbed the handle with both hands and pulled, but the door resisted, feeling stiff. Morgan threw her shoulders and lower back into it, determined to win. She could hear the crackling of sand down in the tracks, creating the obstruction. When the door finally gave, she crossed the threshold and made her way to the wooden railing.

Dangling her upper torso over the side, she noticed stairs off to the left of the deck leading to the beach below. There were tall, jungle-like bushes acting as a privacy fence along the side of the stairway.

The breeze trailing off the ocean hit her face. Closing her eyes, she took in a deep breath. Her cheeks tingled from the crisp air. Realizing that she was losing sunlight, she ran out to the SUV to grab her camera and forage for the bag that contained her clothes.

Like an anxious child, she dashed into the bedroom and emptied the entire bag of clothes onto the floor. Fumbling through the pile, Morgan picked out a white halter top and blue jean cut-off shorts. In a split second, she was donning summer clothes, bypassing the option to wear shoes. Someone had once told her that toes in the sand were an instant pedicure.

Sprinting to the back patio, she scooped up her digital camera along the way and pranced down the steps toward the beach, carefully hanging onto the wooden banister on her way down. Her feet hit the sand, slowing down her stance, allowing an opportunity to secure her camera around her neck. Her ankles made contact with the lapping waves of the ocean and the chilly water stunned her.

Morgan's olive skin and brown hair glistened from the sun that danced right off the top of the ocean. Soon, the sun would disappear into the bottom of the sea. The tide was out, exposing one small tide pool after the other, revealing starfish, sea urchins, and anemones. She prepared her camera, pausing for a moment of clarity. An overwhelming feeling took hold as she realized she was standing in the epicenter of her new journey.

She began her trek across rough rocks that seemed to move beneath her. She laughed out loud when she discovered crabs camouflaged against the rocks. They raced by her creating the illusion. Shaking her head, she began to leap from one tide pool to another looking for willing subjects to photograph.

Seagulls circled above, singing gloriously. Not paying attention to the change in terrain, Morgan lost her footing on a slimy textured rock.

Her right ankle slipped into a crack and twisted uncomfortably. A sharp pain shot through her as she struggled to regain balance. One arm protected her camera while the other flailed in the air to catch her fall. Her arm buckled when she hit the ground, her shoulder and tailbone taking the brunt of the fall.

She lay still to remain calm and evaluate her injuries. Breathing heavily, she took note that she hadn't broken her neck or hit her head. Her ankle throbbed and her back ached from landing on the rocks.

"Shit. Dammit," she groaned.

She slowly raised her upper body to look at her ankle. It appeared normal. She decided to attempt to get up.

"Take it slow … here we go."

Her ankle wasn't having it. She was back down on the ground before she knew it. Looking behind her to see how far she'd wandered from the cottage, she noticed there wasn't a soul in sight and she was too far to make it back.

What a mess, she thought.

Morgan had begun to devise a plan when a figure coming at her caught the corner of her eye. What was left of the sun pierced her right in the eyes, and all she could make out was someone tall. A man, she guessed by his silhouette. Her hand came up to block the sun from its blinding rays.

The mystery man crouched beside her. Wearing black aviator sunglasses, he appeared to be staring at her. A cocky grin surfaced at the corner of his mouth as he raised the dark glasses, exposing sexy green eyes. It almost seemed he was laughing at her predicament.

"That wasn't the most graceful scene I've witnessed in a long time," the stranger teased.

Morgan frowned at his arrogant humor but softened a bit at the sight of his gorgeous smile.

"Looks like you could use some help here," he said, offering a hand. "My name is Brody. Brody Mason."

CHAPTER TWO

UNFORESEEN ACCIDENTS/ BLESSING IN DISGUISE

Brody's hand lingered in the air as he waited for Morgan's response. Her eyes locked on Brody's, her mouth dangling open just enough for the drool to surface if she didn't pull herself together—and quick. Clearing her throat, Morgan shook her head to snap out of the state of paralysis.

"Hi ... uh ... this is incredibly embarrassing," she said, reaching out to shake his hand. "I can't believe what I've done here. I think it's just a sprain." She gestured toward her ankle.

Brody moved in closer to assess her condition. Morgan observed him intently. Something about him was familiar. She couldn't quite place it, and it was nagging at her. Brody stood, his six-foot frame towering over her.

"Damn—that's going to hurt like a son of a bitch tonight. I think it's safe to say you aren't walking out of here," he said.

Morgan heard him talking but was completed distracted by his attire and physique. Her eyes scanned up and down his body noting blue jeans, white Converse tennis shoes, and an Alice Cooper concert t-shirt. Everything about him screamed rock 'n' roll, especially his dark messy hair. The kind that projected sexy as opposed to *I haven't washed my hair in a week.*

Brody's eyebrows furrowed. She wasn't listening to a word he said. He was annoyed until he realized she was checking him out. Folding his arms across his chest, he smiled, waiting patiently for her to refocus her attention on the situation at hand.

"Hellooo ... are you with me?" he teased almost arrogantly. Her head jerked back to attention and she felt the embarrassment of getting caught in the act.

"Mmhmm ... yes ... yes, I could probably use some help back to my cottage if it's not a huge inconvenience. By the way, my name is Morgan. Morgan Gray. Thank you for coming over here to offer some assistance."

Unbeknownst to Morgan, he'd been watching her from the moment she stepped onto the beach.

* * *

Brody's home sat up on the cliffs overlooking the ocean. Big shiny windows wrapped around the stunning home with a white deck off the back. A steep paved path lined with rice paper plants and palm trees led to the beach. He was an LA-based musician, and his band Keyed Up often retreated to his Santa Cruz home to work on new material.

Brody had been winding down in the upstairs living room when Morgan had caught his eye. The first thing he'd thought was *Whoa—who's that?* He'd been taken in by her long beautiful legs, but ultimately it was her enthusiasm that had him mesmerized. Her inhibition had brought a smile to his face and Brody found it fascinating. Realizing he was intruding on her private moments, he'd been turning to leave the room when he saw her fall.

Bringing himself back to Morgan's dilemma, he reached out for her hand to help her up.

"Come on. Let's get you home so you can get some ice on that." He looked around to guess which house was hers.

She stood, resting her hands on his chest for balance. She looked up at him and their eyes locked. After what seemed like an eternity, Brody was the first to break the connection. He scooped her up in his arms and said, "Lead the way."

Morgan directed him toward her cottage, and it wasn't long before they met the stairs leading up to the back deck. He carried her up without much effort and gently set her down in front of the sliding-glass door. He took a moment to look around the property.

"I know this place. Been by it a million times. I've never seen you here before, though. Are you ... staying for a while?"

"I have the cottage for the summer. Maybe longer ..." she responded. "I can't thank you enough, Brody." She smiled at him shyly.

Brody bent his head down to stare at the ground as he gathered his thoughts. When his head came back up, those sexy green eyes and cocky grin almost knocked Morgan over.

"Maybe I'll see you around, Morgan. Take care of that foot."

He shot down the stairs and disappeared from her sight within seconds.

It had gotten dark and the chill from the breeze caused her to shiver. Her mind was reeling. Where did she know him from? She opened the sliding-glass door and hobbled into the cottage. Hopping on one foot, she managed to maneuver around the cottage to pour herself a glass of wine, locate some ibuprofen, and plant herself on the overstuffed sofa in the living room. Placing a large throw pillow under her foot to keep it raised, she unconsciously began to channel-surf. She wasn't paying the least bit of attention. All her thoughts were on Brody Mason.

That name ... that name. She knew it somehow—but why? His eyes. That smile.

When Morgan finally made the connection, it was like someone had busted down the front door. Her entire body flew forward from the back of the couch with her hands thrust to the top of her head.

"Brody Mason! Brody Mason from Keyed Up! How can I be so stupid?" she yelled out. Her heart was pounding out of her chest.

"I was just rescued by Brody Mason. And I didn't even know it."

CHAPTER THREE

MAGNETS PULLING TOWARD ONE ANOTHER

Each day that had gone by since Morgan's injury, the cabin fever had been closing in on her. The swelling in her ankle had gone down and although it felt fragile, she could walk without discomfort. The pull from the oasis outside her back door had been tormenting her. Her hands twisted with anxiousness as she paced and pondered her next move. Not wanting to waste another moment cooped up in the cottage, she headed for the bedroom with brisk energy.

Throwing on a white sundress, she secured her hair back into a loose ponytail and made her way to the beach with her thirty-five millimeter camera dangling in tow. The salty smell of the ocean hovered in the air. Closing her eyes, she allowed the aroma to filter through her body, feeling inspiration spiral through her veins. An uninvited thought began tapping in. One she'd been fighting for days: Brody Mason.

Morgan's eyes burst open in an effort to snap out of it. She lifted the camera, pausing midway to roam the beach with her probing eyes. The voice inside her head said, *Do NOT look for his house. You don't care. Leave it alone.*

But true romantic that she was, her heart leapt in argument. The nervous pounding spoke to her.

Oh yeah … you want to see him all right. Find a way. Make it happen.

The sunset dancing off the ocean brought Morgan back to her senses. She felt waves splashing up against her ankles. Her head came down to discover seashells shuffling in and out of the tide. She bent down to pick one up, but the strength of the current stole it from her grip, leaving only sand for her to sift through. A starfish trapped in a tide pool had become nearly invisible from the exoskeleton skin protecting it. She put her camera to work, clicking away effortlessly.

She'd been lost in concentration, oblivious to the sea breeze blowing her white dress up like a sail. The sun began to work against her as it made its way behind the ocean wall, leaving Morgan without the light she needed to continue.

Finding the perfect spot to nestle into the sand, she sat down to take advantage of her surroundings and all the inspiration they contributed. She thought of her kids and how much she wished they were there to share this experience with her. Tears began to stream down her face. She couldn't remember the last time she felt so free and completely in control of her life.

* * *

Brody had been working away in his recording studio when he discovered Morgan down on the beach. Turning the lights down a bit, he found a place to get comfortable and enjoy the show. Music had been his passion, but the alluring new neighbor was interestingly distracting.

She unknowingly began seducing Brody, her sundress teasing him as the wind unveiled her beautiful skin. The gracefulness she possessed was bewitching, drawing him into a trance that he didn't want to break out of.

Brody knew his limits and the alarm in his head began firing. He'd made a pact with himself: *no* women who would involve commitment. His career was poison for monogamous relationships. It never worked and people got hurt.

He continued to watch and moved a little closer to the window to get a better look. Squinting curiously while stroking his chin, Brody assessed, wishing what he suspected wasn't true.

Yep, definitely the commitment type. Fuck.

The realization disappointed him, but it had no pull to draw him away from the window where he selfishly spied on Morgan.

* * *

Brody could hear a commotion in the house and knew what the unwanted interruption was. The door to the recording studio flew open and a loud voice intruded.

"Yo, Brody—hey, why the hell are you standing here in the dark, man?" asked Jaxon, the live-wire drummer for the band.

Jaxon flipped the lights back on and grabbed his drumsticks, filling the room with his overflowing energy. With his high-strung demeanor and class-clown attitude, he was often the life of the party. His dark-brown eyes bulged volumes before actually speaking.

"Dude, I'm ready to kick some new album ass here," he announced, walking around the room. His long legs led the way while the rest of his body tried to catch up. As he bent down to beat his drumsticks on every surface he could find, his wavy brown hair fell forward, dancing to his tune. He paused for a moment, recognizing Brody's mood. Hesitantly standing up, he started in.

"Ugh—I know that look. Something has you prickly. What the fuck, man?"

The two of them were like brothers. They spoke honestly and directly to each other.

Brody stood there, arms folded across his chest. Leaning against the wall, he crossed his legs and looked down at the ground. Fucking Jaxon always called him out on his shit. The son of a bitch. The thought made him smirk, then cock a smile. He cranked his head up to respond.

"Just tired, man. Been working all day. Music, lyrics, the usual. Ready to take a break."

Jaxon walked over to Brody, slapping him on the shoulder, "I know that look, and it has *female* written all over it. So ...who is she?"

CHAPTER FOUR

COINCIDENCE OR FATE?

Morgan tapped her pencil back and forth restlessly on the coffee table as she stared out the sliding-glass door. The loneliness was starting to get to her. The only person she'd seen since her arrival to Santa Cruz had been Brody Mason. The thought agitated her. Running into him again had popped into her mind more times than she cared for.

I need to get out. Meet some more people and mingle.

Dropping the pencil, Morgan stood and paced the room. Nail-biting had never been one of her habits, but the thought of venturing out alone in a new town had her nibbling away at her fingertips. Drumming up the courage to go out had her heart pounding. She took her hands away from her mouth and dropped them down into angry fists by her side.

This is ridiculous. Stop overthinking it and just do it.

* * *

After changing into evening wear, Morgan dialed up an Uber ride and was dropped off downtown. It was a beautiful evening as she made her way down the sidewalk, window-shopping and people-watching. The sound of thumping music led her to the front door of a bar and she peeked inside. The place was dark and sultry, with the smell of beer hanging in the air.

Her eyes roamed until she spotted an empty high-top table near the dance floor. A surge of bravery shoved her through the door to snag the table. She took a seat and settled in, contemplating her first drink. Jukebox blaring, she tapped her foot to the beat and began to feel herself loosen up. A young college-type-looking waiter approached her table to take her order.

"Welcome in, ma'am. We have a great lineup of live music tonight. What can I get started for you?"

Ma'am? Ouch—that one hurt. I suppose he isn't going to card me either.

Reeling from the "ma'am" comment, Morgan straightened her shoulders and sat tall. Flashing the waiter a sassy smile, she stepped out of her comfort zone and ordered two shots of tequila. Impressed with her drink choice, the waiter smiled and winked at her.

"Ma'am my ass," she mumbled low, feeling proud of herself.

* * *

Brody had discovered Morgan's arrival in the bar as soon as she took over the high-top table. Kicking back in a chair upstairs overlooking the dance floor, he sipped on a whiskey neat as he observed. His first instinct had been to grab her attention and make his presence known. Oh, but watching was so much fun, so he decided to override the idea.

Brody found himself lost in her beauty. She looked stunning in a cold-shoulder low-cut burgundy dress with a long gold necklace that fell perfectly between her breasts. A shimmering sparkle bounced off the necklace whenever she shifted, teasing and taunting him. His eyes trailed down her long bare legs to the sexy straps that hugged her ankles from her tan wedge high-heeled shoes.

He sat fascinated as Morgan threw back the first shot of tequila. Tapping the shot glass down, she swiftly placed the lime in between her teeth, sucking in the juice. She licked her lips, drawing a finger up to wipe the corner of her mouth. Damned if he wasn't turned on and wanted to lick those lips himself. He'd been so consumed with her, he hadn't even noticed how the entire bar had filled with patrons waiting for the live music to begin.

As the jukebox rested, the lights dimmed throughout the bar. The crowd shuffled to move closer to the stage, whistling and clapping. The band fired up the rock 'n' roll like an explosion, prompting everyone to their feet. Morgan watched as people bounced in front of her, pumping their arms to the beat of the music. She hopped off her chair and blended her way in with the crowd.

Brody hovered from above, leaning over the railing to keep an eye on Morgan. She appeared uninhibited, moving her body carefully to the music in an effort to protect her ankle. Loud sirens were going off in Brody's head. He had an instinct for trouble—the female kind. Pushing himself away from the railing, he headed for his table and signaled the waiter for another round of whiskey.

Brody glanced back at the dance floor and his blood boiled. Some asshole was trying to move in on Morgan. Her body language wasn't encouraging, and Brody could tell she was uncomfortable. Brody slammed the Jameson and took off down the stairs, forcing his way through the thick layer of people on the dance floor until he found Morgan. He grabbed her hand and pushed the asshole away from her.

She could only see him from behind and missed the daggers from his eyes warning the stranger to back the fuck off.

"Brody?" she said.

Tugging on her arm, Brody didn't say a word as he led her off the dance floor. She followed the steps of his white Converse, resting the other hand on the back of his black Rock Revival t-shirt. The grip he had on her suggested she was in trouble.

Is he mad at me? Just who does he think he is? Her heart pounded.

Climbing the stairs with brisk strides to reach the top floor, Brody stopped at his table and let go of Morgan's hand. He turned around to face her, his green eyes piercing. At first she thought she saw rage, but she felt relieved when he reached out to gently rest his hands on her shoulders.

"Are you all right? I saw that guy moving in on you and—" He paused, trying to drum up an ounce of patience.

He felt her shoulders relax as a faint smile surfaced. For a moment, it had crossed his mind that a sharp slap across the face might be her reaction instead.

"I'm fine. Just trying to catch up with what just happened. Umm … thank you … once again." she said.

Their eyes locked onto each other.

Come on, Brody. Don't leave me hanging here, Morgan thought. She didn't want to leave but couldn't think of a reason to stay.

She was first to break the trance. Her head dropped to observe the shuffling of her feet. Awkward fidgeting in an uncomfortable circumstance. Her arms came up to her waist as she looked back up at Brody.

"I'd better make my way back home now. Sorry for the trouble, Brody."

Brody kept his cool and fought the temptation to invite her back to his place.

She turned, pivoting on the heel of her foot with frustration. Grabbing the railing, she started down the stairs. She could feel his eyes on her backside. Little did she know he was admiring the way her dress moved with her hips.

"Morgan …wait," he said, following her down the stairwell.

He stopped and hovered above her.

"The rest of the band is arriving tomorrow from LA. We're throwing a party tomorrow night to kick off the summer and the work ahead of us. Why don't you come by and join us, meet the rest of the band. Say five o'clock?"

Taking a step down to get closer to Morgan, Brody reached out to tuck a piece of hair behind her ear. He smiled and looked into her eyes.

Her lips opened to respond, distracting his attention. She could see that his eyes were on her mouth and she longed for it to be an invitation.

Clearing her throat, Morgan raised her hand as if something were stuck. She felt flushed due to the butterflies swirling in her stomach.

Brody found her nervous demeanor refreshingly innocent. He'd been accustomed to women throwing themselves at him. Another confirmation that she was different.

"What do you say? My place is at the end of our street."

"All right, Brody. I need some fresh air." She gestured to the front door with her thumb. "I'll see you tomorrow night."

She blew down the stairs and out the front door of the bar, cool air greeting her the moment she stepped outside. Things were heating up with Brody and that had her mind spinning. A summer fling would be a first for her and somewhat out of character. She'd wanted him to kiss her tonight, there was no denying it.

Waving down a taxi, Morgan climbed into the back and leaned her head on the vinyl seat.

Morgan, you'd better know what you're getting yourself into.

CHAPTER FIVE

SO CLOSE YOU CAN ALMOST TOUCH IT

Morgan tapped her nails nervously on the side of the refrigerator door and slammed it shut.

Baked macaroni and cheese it is. The perfect dude food for tonight.

Fumbling through kitchen cupboards, she found an old seventies-style casserole dish. Classic cornflower blue CorningWare with a glass lid to complete the ensemble. Humidity lingered in the air and steam from the boiling water caused her to wave the steeping sweat away from her face as she grated cheese. The oven beeped, preheated. Morgan's wrist swept across her forehead as she loaded the oven with her masterpiece and closed the door.

She considered what would be an appropriate outfit for the evening ahead. She strolled into the bedroom and stood in front of the closet door, her eyes roaming. She'd never been to a party of this caliber before. Her hand came up to caress her stomach.

I feel sick.

Morgan blew out a long slow breath and reached for her navy-blue dress. She carefully laid the dress down on the bed as she rummaged through the dresser drawer for undergarments. She plucked out a strapless bra, then her hands froze over one of her few pairs of lacy underwear. Looking around the room as if someone might catch her, she retrieved the slinky thong between her fingertips and held it up high to study it. Then, she turned to look under her armpit.

Tossing the garments aside, she headed straight for the bathroom to shower and shave. She ran her hands up and down her legs, feeling for any prickly spot left untouched.

After slipping on the navy dress, she shifted to adjust the lacy thong.

I'm so not used to this. Feels like a flipping wedgie.

The dress was cut above the knees and swept gently off her shoulders. Tying it all together with a tan belt and nude sandals, she curled her hair and placed gold hoop earrings into her ears. She'd never been one to wear a load of makeup. A little black eyeliner and mascara would do the trick. Dabbing a small drop of perfume to the side of her neck, she set the fragrance down and stared at herself in the mirror.

What am I walking into tonight? Drugs? Groupies? This evening could totally traumatize me.

She was attracted to Brody, but was she really cut out to hook up with a rock star? What if he'd only invited her over tonight to be a nice neighbor?

The scent and sizzling sound of the macaroni and cheese caught her attention, drawing her away from her lecturing reflection. Cheese bubbled as she removed the casserole dish, placing a glass lid on top. She carefully carried it out to her SUV, placing it on the floorboard. She ran back inside the cottage and grabbed a bottle of red wine and her car keys.

She closed the front door behind her then rested her back against it, hesitant to leave. Words such as *coward, chicken,* and *pathetic* drifted through her mind. She felt glued to the front door, legs paralyzed.

Come on, Morgan. You shaved your legs for this.

She reached back and pushed herself away from the door. A few determined strides and she was in her SUV heading toward Brody's house.

As she pulled into the driveway of brick pavers, she slowed down to park under a white pergola with green vines. The home sat secluded among tropical flowers with large leaves and bamboo. She stepped out of the SUV and approached the front door, admiring pink lilies along the way. Holding tightly to her bottle of wine, she rang the doorbell, shifting nervously back and forth from heel to toe. When the door opened, a young man the exact image of Brody greeted her.

"Hey, you must be Morgan. Please, come on in. Can I help you with anything?"

"Yes ... hello ... I have a casserole to bring in. I'll just hand over my wine to you and ... please excuse my flustered demeanor. You've got to be related to Brody."

"Oh shit. I'm sorry. I'm Brody's son, Dylan." He reached out to shake Morgan's hand.

"The kitchen is right through there. I'll get your casserole and be right back. Make yourself at home. Dad should be around here somewhere."

Morgan found her way to the kitchen, exploring every inch and detail. As she set the bottle of red wine down on the dark granite countertop, she heard a commotion from the back patio and began to wander that way when a familiar sexy voice stopped her.

"Hey ... you made it." Brody said.

Dressed in his usual blue jeans and white Converse, Brody dressed things up with a black long-sleeved shirt that buttoned down the front, left untucked. He rolled up the sleeves for a more casual look and wore a silver chain low around his neck. His dark textured hair drew out the intense green of his eyes. Morgan could make out a tiny hint of chest hair and the whole package had her raging with desire.

Brody grabbed her hand and led her into the living room. She took a moment to look around, deciphering his personality by his decor. Her attention became drawn to a large window in the corner of the room and she headed straight for it. From where she stood, it felt like she was standing right on the water. Brody walked up behind her and stepped close enough to speak into her ear.

"Beautiful, isn't it?"

She felt his breath on her neck and a chill flowed through her body, causing her to shiver. Clearing her throat, she turned around to look up at him.

"It's absolutely stunning," she said, a soft smile lifting the corner of her mouth.

She couldn't take her eyes off his. Her lips parted open as she swallowed, trying to find words to break the silence between them.

Brody could sense how nervous she was. He was used to aggressive women and found her innocent behavior intriguing.

His eyes narrowed in on Morgan's mouth as he stepped closer to her. She felt her heart racing with anticipation as Brody moved in to close the gap. Taking note that she didn't step away from him, he continued to make his move. He ran his hand through her soft curls to support the back of her head. Morgan took in a deep breath, ready to succumb.

"Brody! What the hell, man. Get your ass out here!" An annoyed voice approached the living room.

"Oh shit. Sorry man. Guess my timing fucking sucks." The amused intruder stood there, hands on his hips, wearing a tight white tank undershirt and blue jeans that hung just below his white boxer briefs.

"Jaxon," Brody whispered under his breath, looking at Morgan in an apologetic way.

Brody stepped back from Morgan and gave his pal a look that said *Thanks a lot, you asshole.*

"Jaxon. This is my neighbor, Morgan Gray."

Morgan walked over to Jaxon and offered her hand. He had long brown wavy hair and needed about twenty more pounds of muscle.

Brody came up behind her and rested his hand along her back. The gesture pleased Morgan and communicated to Jaxon she was "hands off."

"Jaxon is our drummer. And he's quite the wise guy, as you may have noticed. " He looked at his friend with a smirk. Jaxon's eyes were wide and danced in a way that said *Nice* and *I approve.*

"Dude, drinks are flowing and the babes want to go skinny-dipping. You guys are missing everything. Morgan, you and Mr. Uptight here need a drink. This is supposed to be a fucking *party!*"

"Let's join the others and you can meet the rest of the band," Brody suggested to Morgan.

"Hell yeah," Jaxon said.

"We'll follow you, Jaxon. Lead the way," Morgan insisted, laughing at his goofy stance.

* * *

Loud music and laughing voices led the way to the rest of the group. There was splashing from the pool and the sound of bottle caps popping off beer bottles. An abundance of food, including Morgan's mac and cheese, covered the patio table. She spotted a bottle of champagne chilling and headed straight for it. She picked up a stemless champagne glass and allowed herself a generous pour of the dancing bubbles.

After taking in a few sips, she felt the anxiety go down and decided to put herself out there. She didn't want Brody to babysit her all night. She made her way to the pool area and kicked off her sandals in the corner.

She scanned the crowd to get the lay of the land. Dylan and a young cute blonde were in the hot tub flirting. There were guys and gals in the pool playing chicken, and to her relief, they still had their bathing suits on.

Morgan wasn't aware of it but Brody was mingling with guests, all the while watching her every move. He was curious how she'd blend in with this crowd. It had to be a different experience than what she was used to. Things were calm now and Brody knew it wouldn't stay that way much longer. This was Brody's world, and he had no intention of changing it.

He was subtle but continued to observe Morgan as she made her way over to Nate and Johnny, the remaining members of Keyed Up.

Oh God, please don't act like a couple of dip shits, he thought, brows furrowing inward.

Morgan laughed and gracefully sipped her champagne. Nate and Johnny seemed completely charmed by her, hanging on every word.

Brody excused himself and made his way toward the motley crew that would no doubt be hitting on Morgan at any minute. He approached the group and stood next to her, glaring at Nate and Johnny.

"Uh ... hey, Brody. Morgan was just telling us about how the two of you met. Way to go, man." Nate said.

Nate, the band's lead singer, could belt out some kick-ass rock 'n' roll, but with his sand-colored hair bleached out from the sun and his aqua eyes, he looked more like a surfer. The women loved him and he fed off their attention.

Johnny was about to speak when a lady's wet bathing suit landed across his chest, spraying small mists of water into the air.

"Johnny! We're awfully lonely in here and getting impatient," a woman's voice came from the pool. Her dark hair dripped as she covered her large silicone breasts with her arms, eyelashes batting a mile a minute.

Johnny had muscles the size of the Hulk's, and when he played bass they blew up even more. Removing the bikini top from his chest, he draped it over his black faux-hawk and ran for the pool, plunging in cannonball style. Nate followed, multitasking as he walked and removed his swim trunks at the same time. One bathing suit after the other began surfacing the pool deck.

During all the commotion, Morgan had lost sight of Brody. Not wanting to get suckered into skinny-dipping, she discreetly worked her way back into the house.

* * *

That was close. Morgan closed the sliding-glass door.

She walked into the kitchen to locate her bottle of red wine, feeling the need for another drink. To her relief, Brody wasn't naked in the pool with *them*. But where had he gone? She was fumbling through the drawers to find a wine-bottle opener when she stopped short. Suddenly, all the lights had gone out.

"What the heck?" she whispered, looking around. She could hear footsteps coming from behind her.

"It's just me, Morgan," Brody said softly.

She closed the drawers and felt him standing right behind her. Both of his hands came up and rested on top of her bare shoulders. She took in a deep breath and let it out slowly. Brody leaned his head down and began kissing the tip of her right shoulder, gradually working his way to the base of her neck. She tilted her head to the side ever so slightly to allow access. Everything inside her was tingling.

"Brody ..." Morgan sighed as she turned around to face him.

Their mouths met instantly and she threw her arms around his neck, pulling him in. Brody picked her up and set her down on top of the kitchen counter. With unconscious effort, her legs wrapped around his waist, squeezing him tight. He cupped the back of her head for support while penetrating his tongue deeper. Her hand came up to push against his chest. Then her head drew back as she shifted nervously on the countertop, concerned people were watching.

"Brody, this isn't a scene I'd like Dylan to walk into," she said quietly.

His breathing slowed and those green eyes stared into hers with desire. The force of Brody's arms around her came quickly as he pulled her off the countertop and carried her to another room. He set her down gently.

Morgan stood before him in his bedroom. A king-size steel four-poster bed caught her attention. A charcoal-gray goose-down comforter with large black decorative pillows lay atop the sultry-looking bed.

Who wouldn't want to fuck in that? Morgan thought.

Her eyes investigated the room as any nosy female would. Thoughts of betrayal intruded as she remembered her late husband. Ever since his passing, she'd avoided involvement with men, staying focused on her children. There'd been opportunities—family and friends continually trying to set her up.

Her hand came up to smooth the stress and confusion pumping from her forehead.

Brody stood back, hands on his hips as he watched her. Intuitive enough to realize her mind was somewhere else, he allowed her the time she needed despite the hard-on ready to burst through his blue jeans.

The moment of silence caused Brody to reflect on some matters as well. Things had taken off like a brushfire with Morgan back in the kitchen. She had no idea the asshole he could really be. Morgan wasn't like the women he usually hooked up with. She carried herself with class and integrity and deserved better than a one-night stand.

The hard truth was, Brody never cared about the girls he fucked. In fact, he picked them that way. Getting laid was easy and he didn't care if he ever saw them again. He wanted nothing more than to fuck Morgan for hours but feared the expectations she'd have following. And—damn it all to hell—he cared.

"Morgan …"

Embarrassed, Morgan turned to face Brody. As soon as their eyes met, all guilt and doubt diminished like a vanquished demon. She smiled and began to loosen the belt to her dress. Brody stepped closer to her and laid his hand on hers to stop her from completing the task. His mouth came down on hers, kissing her apologetically, as his hands stroked the side of her arms. Morgan could feel the change in his demeanor and knew she was about to be rejected.

"Maybe we should slow things down a bit, Morgan. I just—"

Morgan's index finger came up and rested on Brody's lips before he could finish his sloppy excuse.

"It's okay, Brody. We're both out of our element here. I … uh … I think we just got a little carried away. I mean, we barely know each other."

"Actually, the thing is—" Brody said, trying to explain.

It was obvious she didn't really get what was going on. This was a noble move for Brody and when it came to women, noble was not his standard behavior.

Motioning for the bedroom door, Morgan kept her chin up while discreetly making a run for it. She stopped in the doorway and her hand grabbed the side casing and gripped tight.

"I'm going to take off, Brody. Thank you for inviting me here. It was no doubt a once-in-a-lifetime experience."

Fuck, Brody thought, following her out the door.

He insisted on walking her out to her SUV and opened the car door as she slid in. Bending down to poke his head in the window, he was about to speak when her cell phone went off.

"Um, Brody. I really have to go. This is my daughter Ashley calling. Thank you—really." She swiped the phone to answer.

Brody stepped back and watched her slowly drive away.

How is it possible I feel like the biggest dick when I was just trying to do the right thing? Fuck! He stood on the brick pavers, perplexed.

"Dad, who are you talking to out here?" Dylan asked, standing in the entryway.

"How long have you been there?" Brody questioned.

"Not long. Everyone's looking for you. Pull yourself out of your senior moment and get back in here. It's a party, remember?" Dylan slammed the door shut.

"Nice," Brody mumbled.

CHAPTER SIX

ATTRACTION, TEMPTATION, AND CAVING IN

"There's something missing in that last verse. It isn't flowing right. Jaxon, I think the beat needs to slow down a bit," Brody suggested.

Nate paced around the recording studio, hands resting on top of his head, trying to be patient. The band had been working endless hours, fighting fatigue and restraining themselves from killing each other. Johnny plucked away on his bass, his black faux-hawk bouncing to the rhythm, as the rest of the band tried to cool down. Dylan stepped out of the sound booth, headphones dangling from his fingers. Shutting the door behind him, he surveyed the mood in the room.

"You guys look fucking whipped. Let's wrap things up and take a break." he said.

At the young age of twenty-two, Dylan had become the band's right hand. A musician himself, he'd taken on the role of recording and management. Being raised in the industry had taught him everything he needed to know, including the scandalous side Brody had tried to shelter him from growing up. By the time Dylan was ten, he could play multiple instruments, making it evident he'd follow in his Dad's footsteps.

Brody had been the workaholic of the group and expected a lot from the others. If he wasn't careful, the guys would get burnt out, leading to havoc. There had been no women or booze for several days.

"Dylan's right. Let's shut things down and get the fuck out of here," Brody said, setting his guitar down.

Jaxon stood, throwing his drumsticks into the air. "Oh hell yes!"

Santa Cruz on a Saturday night was promising. In and out of dive bars, it didn't take long for the guys to have blondes and brunettes hanging on their arms like accessories. Prowling the streets for the next bar to patronize, Jaxon noticed Brody looking uninterested in the ready-and-willing women following his every move.

"Dude. What the fuck is your problem? You're treating that blonde bombshell like a disease or something. Do you want to get laid tonight or what, man?" Jaxon said.

Just in that moment, someone had caught Brody's eye through the window of a bougie restaurant. Leaning his head against the glass, he attempted to get a closer look. A woman in a black cocktail dress sat at the bar sipping a martini, her brown hair pinned back with tendrils flowing loosely down her bare back. She wore spiked high heels with rhinestones shimmering off the top. The mystery lady turned slightly toward the window, giving Brody a better visual.

A jolt shot through him and he backed away from the window. The elegant woman at the bar was Morgan Gray. He hadn't seen her for a few weeks, but he'd been thinking of her.

"Fuck off, Jaxon. I'll catch up with you guys in a minute." Brody said, opening the door to the restaurant.

The second Brody stepped inside, it was obvious this wasn't his usual venue. Everything shined and sparkled, with white table clothes and fresh flowers. No beer stench to be found. His attention diverted to Morgan's laughter as she conversed with the not-so-bad-looking bartender. Jealousy came over him. He didn't like Morgan being there, especially looking like *that*.

With annoyed determination, he moved swiftly to take a seat next to Morgan. The mild scent of her perfume drifted through his senses.

"How ya doing? What can I get for you this evening?" the bartender asked, acknowledging Brody's arrival.

"Jameson, neat."

Morgan recognized his voice and spun her barstool around to face him.

"Brody ... hey," she said, trying not to express enthusiasm.

"Hey. Just out for a casual evening, I see?" Brody said, green eyes narrowing at her.

Morgan shifted in her seat, feeling uncomfortable.

Oh no you don't, mister. You're not going to intimidate me this time.

Sitting straight and tall to exude confidence, Morgan responded.

"I wanted to get out and be social. Have some fun." She glared at him with a look that said *What's it to you, anyway?*

Receiving the message loud and clear, Brody smiled, amused by her sass, and he decided to stand down. He hadn't intended on picking a fight with her. Jealousy was rearing its ugly head and it wasn't flattering. He flashed his sexy smile and moved in closer to her, placing his arm across her bare back. She stiffened at his touch.

"Ouch—a little prickly, are we?" Brody said.

Morgan's head jerked to look him in the eye.

"I'm just not in the neighborly mood, Brody."

"And salty too …" he said, his smile faltering.

The look on Brody's face got to Morgan. This wasn't who she truly was. He'd wounded her ego, catapulting her into defense mode.

Brody threw ten bucks on the bar and swiveled his barstool to leave. Morgan reached out to grab his hand.

"Brody, wait. Please stay. Let's … try again."

He sat back down and ordered another whiskey neat.

Drinks were flowing, lightening the mood, and Morgan soon forgot about being sore with him.

Resting his hand on her thigh, he filled her in on the work the band had accomplished over the last few weeks. She accepted the endearment, hopeful he'd changed his mind about "slowing things down." The longer they talked, the closer their bodies moved toward each other. Morgan raised her hand to stroke the back of his neck.

"Brody, about the night of the party. I think we should—"

A disturbance rumbled through the restaurant before she could finish. Jaxon stumbled through the front door, loud and drunk.

"Brody—shit, man. We've been waiting all night for you. Morgan? Damn, girl. You look smokin' hot tonight." Jaxon slapped Brody on the side of the back.

Morgan smiled, glancing at the two women hanging on Jaxon like he was a Greek God. A voluptuous brunette had one arm looped around Jaxon's arm as she leaned in close to Brody's ear.

"Brody, aren't you going to come out and play?" she said in a pouty voice.

Excuse me? Morgan thought, her eyes widening. *Is she really hitting on him right in front of me?*

Morgan glanced at Brody, who appeared completely aloof.

"Brody is currently occupied, so you can go *play* with someone else," Morgan said, picking up her martini glass to slam the dregs. The clinking sound of the glass, as she set it down on the bar, projected attitude. She looked at the brazen brunette, challenging her.

"Jaxon, let's get out of here. This place is a drag." the brunette whined.

"We're out, Brody. Catch you guys later." Jaxon said.

Morgan kept her eyes on the threesome as they left the restaurant. Turning back to Brody, she wondered if she'd overstepped.

"That may have been presumptuous and over the line, Brody." she admitted.

He smiled, then moved in to kiss her on the lips.

"I thought it was fucking perfect."

He got up from his stool and threw a wad of cash at the bartender. Grabbing Morgan's hand, he escorted her out of the restaurant and waved a car down. His own personal limo, no less.

As soon as they slid in, he pulled her onto his lap, kissing and touching her. She felt his hand lift the hem of her dress, slipping in to stroke up and down the side of her leg. His fingers brushed the side of her panties, causing Morgan to anticipate his next move. Breathing heavily, Morgan allowed him access underneath the silk sheath.

Brody could feel how ready she was for him and it nearly sent him over the edge. Removing his hand from under her dress, he latched on to her hip, squeezing tight.

"If we don't slow down, Morgan, I'm going to take you right here. We're almost home." Brody said.

He looked out the car window, relieved they were pulling into the drive.

Morgan slid off his lap and readjusted her dress. Brody had the door open before the car had completely stopped. His long legs stepped out and he reached for Morgan's hand.

He guided her through the house, assessing whether or not they were home alone. Tiptoeing toward his bedroom, he took note that the house was unusually quiet.

"Jaxon is definitely *not* here. I think we're good." he said, peeking out the hall of his bedroom door.

The full moon glistened through the sliding-glass door, enhancing every angle of their silhouettes. Morgan slipped off her high-heeled shoes, tossing them onto the floor. Brody stood in front of the four-poster bed as she approached.

Grabbing the hem of his red Reclaim t-shirt, Morgan slowly slipped it over his head. Her hands came up to rest on Brody's chest, feeling the texture of his skin. A long silver chain hung from around his neck, settling at the edge of her fingertips.

She began to walk around him, the touch of her hand never leaving his body. She stopped to stand behind Brody, placing gentle kisses from the top of his spine to the bottom. He quickly turned around and planted his mouth on hers.

"You've been teasing me all night in that damn dress and now it's time for it to come off," Brody demanded as he began unzipping the black sheath.

The dress slid down her body to her ankles. He knelt to remove her panties, kissing every inch of her leg along the way. Resting her hands on his bare shoulders, she assisted, lifting her feet.

He stood to pick her up and carry her to his bed. Pulling back the gray comforter and sheets, he laid her down and she could feel herself sink into the soft mattress. She watched closely as he removed his shoes and blue jeans. Grabbing a condom from the nightstand, he dressed his arousal and slid into the bed next to her.

Within seconds, her hands were tangled through his hair, pulling him closer to her mouth. Thrusting his tongue inside, he shifted his body to lay above hers. Her legs spread open to wrap around him like a glove. He couldn't wait any longer to penetrate, his rhythm sensually slow. Morgan's hips moved with his, the desire building tempo as he thrust harder and harder. She lifted her body to get closer, wrapping her arms around Brody tighter. He could feel her breasts against his chest.

"Brody—" she whispered, sounding breathless.

"Oh God, not yet, baby."

His thrusting paused as he flipped her over to get her on top of him. Morgan's legs straddled his sides and she readjusted herself over his shaft. His hands came up to cup her breasts as she pumped up and down, driving him inside her. Her head fell back as she arched to project her breasts closer to his hands. The ends of her hair tickled her bare back as he groped and massaged.

"Morgan, fuck!" Brody said, his orgasm exploding like a rocket taking off.

Morgan collapsed on top of his chest, hearing his pulsing heartbeat and feeling it *thump, thump, thump*. His hand came up to stroke the back of her head as his body recovered. He kissed the top of her head and rolled her onto her back.

He slipped his hand down to stroke her clit, working magic with his fingers against her sweet spot. Drawing her knees up, she arched her hips closer to his fingers for more pressure. Her hands came up to squeeze the sides of the pillow as the feeling intensified. Her breathing increased and he felt her pulsate against his hand.

"That was … that was … so good," she said.

He laughed, kissing her temple.

"Glad I didn't disappoint. I'll be right back. Just give me a sec," he said.

Morgan pulled the covers up over her body and pondered the inevitable. Would Brody want her to stay the night, or should she go home? It had been so long since she'd dated or made love to a man. She hadn't missed the awkward moments and relationship games.

Brody came out of the bathroom holding a glass of water and offered it to Morgan. He was still naked, obviously very comfortable with nudity. She took a sip and set the glass down on the nightstand, self-consciously keeping the covers draped over her bare breasts.

"Brody—" she started.

"Scoot over, Morgan. I'm whipped. I think you intended on killing me tonight."

He lay next to her, draping his arm across her stomach.

Well okay, she thought, relieved.

* * *

The following morning, Morgan was first to wake. Brody was still nestled close and she could hear his steady breathing and feel the rise and fall of his chest. Her hand slowly lifted the covers as she attempted to slip out of bed without waking him. His arm shot out to wrap around her stomach, reeling her back into the bed.

"Where do you think you're going?" he asked in a playful tone.

"Brodyyyy—I have to pee." Morgan laughed.

She picked up his red t-shirt off the floor and slipped it over her head, covering her upper body. Brody admired the slight exposure of her butt cheeks as she walked into the bathroom.

Shutting the door behind her, Morgan browsed around the bathroom, searching for items she could freshen up with. She picked up a bottle of Brody's cologne, removed the silver cap, and took a sniff. She closed her eyes, her senses tingled at the familiar fragrance. She opened a drawer and found a hairbrush, thrilled to comb the tangles out of her brown strands.

Finishing her business, she slowly opened the bathroom door to take a peek. Brody was nowhere to be found, but the scent of coffee drifted in the air, invigorating her. Following the scent led her straight to the kitchen, where she found him standing at the counter, wearing blue boxer briefs and holding a coffee mug.

"Good morning," she said, feeling self-conscious about her lack of clothes.

Her eyes roamed, tugging down on the red t-shirt to cover herself just in case Jaxon or the others were around.

"Don't worry. We're alone. How about some coffee?" Brody said, amused by her shy behavior. "Let's have our coffee on the patio. It's gorgeous out."

Morgan followed him out, taking a seat at a table with a large umbrella, hovering to shield them from the sun's piercing rays.

"Shouldn't you be recording this morning? Where is everyone?" Morgan asked.

"I told them to fuck off for a few hours." Brody said.

"You told them to fuck off? Just—Hey! Fuck off you guys— like that?"

"Yep, just like that."

Raising her eyebrows, she took a sip of her coffee. Wow.

"The other day you mentioned a daughter," Brody said. "Ashley was it? How many kids do you have?"

"Three children. Justin and Ashley live in Denver, and Brooklyn just moved to Venice Beach. They're all coming out next weekend for a visit. I, um ... lost my husband eight years ago."

Brody looked at her in surprise. What a tragic loss—and at such a young age.

"I'm truly sorry, Morgan. Eight years ... and never remarried, or?"

"No ... No. I've been lonely at times, of course, but I just really wanted to focus on my kids. Now that the kids are grown and have moved on to live their own lives, I realized I needed to make some goals for myself. I sold our home and packed up to live here for the summer, and then ... well, I have some time to figure that out. I have my camera and we'll see where it takes me."

He listened intently, nodding in agreement to her every word.

"Moving on is important, Morgan. You're so young and there's so much life to be lived." Brody said.

He picked up her hand and kissed the inside of her palm. He couldn't help but wonder if he was the first man she'd made love to in eight years. Not that it mattered to his ego ... well, maybe a little.

"Morgan, my career sets certain limits for the type of relationships I can have. Dylan's my only child and I really tried to make things work with his mom. We never married ... but I was devoted. The thing is, in my line of work, there are always women around, and I'm traveling several months throughout the year. It's a toxic lifestyle. But it's my passion and I'll continue to make music and perform as long as I can."

"I get it. I have absolutely no expectations from you, Brody. The last thing I was looking for when I came out to Santa Cruz was a relationship. We don't need to get into the heavy. I'd love to spend more time with you, no strings attached, if you'd like that too. All I ask is no bullshit, Brody. We're way too old for games and I won't do it."

Brody couldn't believe what he'd just heard. It took a lot of courage to speak so honestly. But did she really mean it? No strings? Women always had strings.

She stood and leaned down to kiss him.

"I'm going to grab my clothes and head home before Jaxon shows up. Don't be a stranger, Brody."

CHAPTER SEVEN

There's Always Tomorrow

MORGAN sat on her living room sofa, leaning over the coffee table and sorting through the photographs she'd developed of her work. Critiquing each one, she jotted down details on a notepad of what she'd missed, highlighting in blue the more appealing aspects. Picking up her camera, she began inspecting the lens features, peering in and out, concentrating on proper focus.

A light *tap, tap, tap* from the sliding-glass door caused her to jump. Her hand flew up to her chest in relief when she discovered the disturbance was Brody. He stood outside, smiling devilishly for having scared her. She narrowed her eyes at him, shaking her head as she opened the door.

"You scared the crap out of me, Brody. Come on in."

It had been several days since Morgan had seen Brody. The fact that he took the initiative to see her today made her do a party dance inside.

"What do you have going on over here?" he asked, noticing the pile of pictures on the table.

"This is some of my work since I arrived in Santa Cruz. I'm proofing the photos, figuring out what I like, what I missed, and how I can do things better."

"Right ... your photography. May I take a look?" He bent down to pick up one of the photos.

Before she could respond, he had one in his hand, inspecting it closely. She chewed nervously on the tip of her fingernail as she waited for him to say something. He was quiet for a few moments, then turned to her.

"This is nice work, Morgan. I like the detail you captured." he said, sounding genuine.

"Thank you ... um ... can you stay for a while? I was just about to kick back on the beach with a glass of wine and watch the sunset." Her hands slipped into the back pockets of her blue jeans, anxious for him to accept.

She wore a white blouse tied in a knot above her navel and buttoned low between her breasts. The subtle cleavage caught Brody's eye, firing off thoughts of bending her over the couch right then and there.

"If you have beer, I'm in," he responded.

"All right, then. Just give me a second to round stuff up. Can you go grab the beer out of the fridge, please?"

Morgan worked swiftly to pack a basket with a bottle of red wine and a cheap glass. Snatching a blanket off the side of the couch, she led the way, while Brody followed carrying two cans of beer. They made their way along the beach looking for the perfect spot to settle. Brody noticed a large log that had washed up, rendering an ideal backrest. He steered Morgan to it, taking the blanket from her and throwing it down on the sand.

"Our timing is perfect," she said. "It's beautiful out right now. Just look how the sun reflects off the glassiness of the water. It mesmerizes me." She lowered herself to lean against the dried-out log.

Brody fumbled through the basket and pulled out the wine glass and bottle.

"Morgan, there's no wine opener in here."

"That's because it's a screw cap." She lifted an eyebrow facetiously.

"Since when did they start making bottles like this?" He twisted off the cap and filled her glass with a generous pour.

He handed her the glass as he bent down to sit next to her. He popped open his can of beer and took a sip, draping his arm across her thigh.

She felt relaxed and comfortable, and it only seemed natural for her to rest her head against his shoulder.

"We have a title for our new album," he said. "*Behind Closed Doors*. What do you think?"

Morgan raised her head to respond, feeling honored he'd ask her opinion.

"I think it's perfect. Very rock 'n' roll." she said.

The wine flowed through Morgan's system like an aphrodisiac. All she could think about was kissing him, touching him, and more. All inhibition disappeared as she set her wine glass down and straddled his lap. Brody's arms came around her back, pulling her closer. His response told Morgan he wanted her, too. His lips found hers and both her hands ravaged through his dark hair.

With an urge for more, she broke off the kiss to escalate the connection.

"Brody, let's go back to my place." she said.

He paused for a moment to look into her eyes, brushing a few hair strands away from her cheeks. A subtle breeze drifted through them, creating a slight cool-down from the friction of heat they'd generated. Brody lifted Morgan off his lap, stood up, and reached down for her hand. He pulled her up and they began packing up their belongings to head back to her cottage.

Morgan looked around the beach, a distant sound pulling at her.

"Do you hear that, Brody? It sounds like someone's yelling," she said, concerned.

She walked toward the sound of the voices, concentrating. Brody stood in place, hands on his hips, curious at her fascination.

Morgan sucked in a quick breath and her hands flew up to her mouth.

"Oh my God!" she said, then chuckled.

Brody strolled up behind her, "What's going on?"

Removing her hands from her mouth, she turned around to look at him with a shy grin.

"My kids are here—a day *early*."

Brody's eyes shot wide open with surprise.

"Are you fucking kidding me?" he asked, panicked.

This was *not* the time to meet Morgan's kids. He had a hard-on bigger than a baseball bat. Wouldn't *that* make a great impression.

"Uh … no offense, sweetheart—I cannot meet your kids like this," he pleaded, gesturing toward his erection.

"I'm so sorry, Brody," Morgan said, laughing at his predicament.

Looking over at the deck of her cottage, she could see her kids wondering about trying to find her.

"I'd better go before they discover us," she said, standing on tiptoe to kiss him goodnight.

He couldn't help but watch as she walked away.

"Shit," he moaned under his breath.

Running a hand through his hair in frustration, he turned on his heels to walk home.

* * *

Ashley, Brooklyn, and Justin dangled over the patio deck searching for their mom. Justin spotted someone waving their arms at them.

"There she is! Mom!" He waved back at her. Ashley and Brooklyn barreled down the stairs to catch up to Morgan on the beach.

"Hey, what a nice surprise! You guys weren't supposed to be here until tomorrow." Morgan reached her arms out to embrace them.

"We wanted to surprise you, Mom," Ashley said.

Morgan felt touched and smiled at her daughters endearingly. They climbed their way back up the patio stairs, where Justin waited anxiously at the top. Morgan reached the last step and walked right into his arms. He held her tight and spoke softly. "Hey Mom."

Justin stood five ten with brown hair and hazel-green eyes. He was always well groomed, hair and clothes perfect. He was the spitting image of a model out of Abercrombie & Fitch.

"You look handsome as always, Justin. Denver is treating you well. Let's all go inside and get caught up." She escorted them into the small cottage.

They had dinner in and watched movies until sleep defeated them. Morgan stood up to make her way to the bedroom. A smile flooded her face when she looked over at her grown children. All three were cuddled on the couch, lying like a family of ferrets. Legs over legs, with heads leaning on one another. She picked up her camera and took several shots of the heartwarming scene.

When she finally made it into her own bed for the night, thoughts of Brody took over. She'd longed to make love to him again. Closing her eyes, she drifted off to sleep fantasizing about his mouth on hers. She could literally taste his tongue.

* * *

The following day, Morgan and her kids spent time down at the beach. Brooklyn and Ashley were sprawled out on beach towels, working on their tans. The day was beautiful with plentiful sunshine assisting their desires. Justin, who had a hard time putting work aside, was in a chair under an umbrella, punching numbers into his laptop. Morgan admired his dedication and never said a word but secretly hoped he wouldn't work all weekend.

She strolled along the beach just far enough for the tide to flood over the top of her feet. Beach combing had kept her busy, and she'd been clueless about her surroundings. From the corner of her eye, she could see Brody's house and tried to discipline herself not to look.

Great. Now I'm a stalker. That person who subconsciously, not on purpose, wants to be seen. And not just by anyone. By a certain tall, green-eyed, sexy-as-hell rock star living in the house above the cliffs.

Embarrassed, she quickly turned to walk back toward her cottage.

"I thought we could all head down to the boardwalk after a while," she suggested when she reached the kids.

Brooklyn's head raised swiftly from the beach towel. "Oh *yes*. I'm down for that."

She'd always been a thrill-seeker, which Morgan admired and dreaded at the same time. Going to the boardwalk with Brooklyn meant finding the courage to get on a roller coaster. Morgan bent down in front of Justin, looking directly into his eyes. He stopped typing to make eye contact with her. He knew exactly what she was thinking. The corner of his mouth curled.

"Yes, Mom. I'll endure some roller coasters with Brooklyn."

Morgan threw her hand across her heart and blew out a breath of relief.

"Oh my God, Justin. Thank you so much. The last time I did the boardwalk thing with Brooklyn, I had to go on every ride with her. And fortunately for me, they were pretty tame compared to the rides at the Santa Cruz boardwalk. She'll love it."

Ashley and Brooklyn packed up their towels and tanning supplies, anxious to clean up and go to the boardwalk. They chatted nonstop all the way back to the cottage, giggling like girlfriends. Morgan followed close behind watching intently. Her daughters had grown up like most sisters do: fighting over every little thing, acting as if they couldn't stand each other. Morgan had always thought of it as a normal phase during their childhood but was secretly concerned it might never change. Now everyone was getting along, enjoying the family time, and Morgan couldn't be happier.

Justin wandered in shortly after them and found a place to put his work away. Being the typical man who only needs three minutes to get ready, he stepped out of the bedroom wearing blue jeans, black Nikes, and a light-blue OBEY-brand t-shirt. Anticipating the UV rays at the boardwalk, he threw on a black-and-white snapback hat. He walked over to the bathroom door listening in to his sisters' nonstop babble.

"Come on you guys," he said, banging on the door with the side of his fist. "You don't need to dress up for the damn boardwalk. It's time to roll out."

He paused and stepped away, shaking his head. Morgan stood inside the entry of the kitchen, leaning against the wall, holding a beer out for him.

"Keep them coming, Mom. We're going to need it this weekend," he pleaded, then tipped his head back to guzzle the amber liquid.

CHAPTER EIGHT

WOMEN, CHILDREN, AND WHISKEY

Dylan pulled into Brody's driveway, easing to a stop while he talked away on his cell phone, the black Escalade purring.

"I need those album-cover proofs ASAP. We're closing in and don't want any hang-ups. Thanks, man."

He turned off the engine, stepped out, and slammed the door behind him. Draping a brown leather cross-body bag over his shoulder, he let himself into Brody's house, heading straight for the recording studio.

From the corner of his eye, he could see Jaxon's clown like movements projecting from the back patio. Shaking his head in wonder, Dylan paused to observe. He'd never known anyone so animated as Jaxon. He was talking with his hands at Brody, most likely trying to get a rise out of him. As usual, Nate and Johnny were in the background egging him on. Dylan changed his course and headed out to the patio to join them.

"What the hell are you assholes doing while I'm out busting my ass?" He walked over to Jaxon and pushed him into the pool.

"Oh shit, Dylan. Now it's going to be like kindergarten camp here," Brody said.

And he was right. Within seconds, Jaxon grabbed Dylan and pulled him into to the pool with him. Nate and Johnny stripped down to their skivvies and cannonballed in, creating a huge splash that struck Brody, soaking him instantly. It was quiet for a brief moment, while the adult adolescents waited with pursed lips to see what Brody's reaction would be. How does one maintain a badass rocker image when he looks like a drowned rat? Dylan tried to hold back his laughter.

Brody knelt to face his perpetrators.

"You guys are buying me all the whiskey I can drink tonight, you sons of bitches." He stared them down, then broke into a shit-eating grin.

* * *

After an exhausting afternoon at the Santa Cruz Boardwalk, Morgan and her kids were gearing up for the evening. She'd made dinner reservations at a restaurant with ocean views and rave reviews.

"Everyone dress their best tonight. This restaurant is supposed to be classy and beautiful," she said.

Brooklyn was the first to emerge from the bathroom. She wore a short black spaghetti-strap dress, complimented by black Vans. Morgan smiled at her beautiful daughter, who had long brown hair that flowed to the middle of her back and hypnotizing crystal-blue eyes.

"Interesting shoe choice, Brooklyn. That is so you."

"Mom, how do I look? Is my dress okay?" Ashley questioned, walking toward Morgan with an unsure look.

She wore a yellow-and-white striped maxi dress that hugged her lean figure. Ashley stood there waiting for her Mom's response while putting gold dangling earrings in. Her features were similar to Morgan's and people often referred to the two of them as twins.

"*Both* of you look so beautiful. You just blow me away," Morgan said.

As Ashley bent down to buckle her tan sandals, Justin wandered in to join them. He worked aggressively with a lint roller up and down his grey pants, making sure to go over his white dress shirt as well.

"You missed a spot," Ashley teased her big brother, who was, in her opinion, a clean freak with OCD tendencies. Justin paused the lint-roller action to inspect, realizing Ashley was being sarcastic.

"Our Uber ride is here. Time to go," Morgan said.

She grabbed her small black clutch and was first out the front door.

The Uber took them on the outskirts of town, turning onto a secluded road. The car climbed the winding road until it finally reached the oasis at the top. Water features and soft Zen music greeted them as they stepped out of the car. A tall gentleman in a tuxedo welcomed their arrival and escorted them inside the restaurant. The maître d' confirmed the reservation and led them directly to the patio dining area. A light breeze drifted through, depositing aromas off the ocean.

"The ocean goes on for miles out there, just like an infinity pool," Brooklyn said, appreciating the views.

There were tropical plants and fluorescent flowers clustered in every nook and cranny. Each group of tables was protected by pergolas that hosted green vines woven throughout. The tables were decorated with burlap runners and mason jars filled with white daisies and floating candles. Simple but ever so inviting. Light music played in the background, enticing couples to sway on the dance floor. The roaring flames from the fire pits and the white twinkle lights that hung around the patio perimeter were perfect props for a seductive ambiance.

* * *

Brody and Dylan were seated near the fire pits sipping whiskey neat.

"What a coincidence that Nate and Johnny had other plans tonight so that they wouldn't have to pay up on drowning me today," Brody said.

Dylan couldn't help but notice how different his dad had been lately. He'd been fun and a little more laid-back than usual. Not so serious and stuffy. He liked this side of his dad. Brody took his work so seriously at times he'd forget to have fun along the way.

Dylan's thoughts were interrupted by the dinner party about to be seated across the way. His eyes raised at the sight of Brooklyn and Ashley and he continued to watch intently. Suddenly his eyes furrowed a bit as he tried to get a closer look.

"Hey, Dad—isn't that Morgan walking in over there?"

Brody swung his head around in eager curiosity. There she was, sure as shit, getting seated at a table with her kids. He sat there and stared as Dylan observed his dad completely fixated on Morgan. She was dressed to kill in dark-blue skinny jeans, a black halter top, and those damn rhinestone stilettos. A slight grin surfaced at the corner of Dylan's mouth. His dad had it *bad*.

"Who's she with? Those chicks are smoking hot." Dylan asked.

"That would be her three kids." Brody took a big swig of his drink. "They're visiting for the weekend."

Slamming the rest of the drink, Brody waved the waiter down for another round.

"No shit. Well, we shouldn't be rude. Let's go over and say hi." Dylan shot off the bench before Brody could respond and made his way over to their table.

"Dylan!" Brody murmured under his breath.

Dylan kept his stride, pretending he didn't hear him.

Well fuck, Brody thought. He had no choice but to go over there now. It wasn't that he didn't want to see Morgan and meet her kids. They'd just never discussed what to tell people about their relationship and he was unsure how to present himself.

Morgan ordered a bottle of sparkling wine for the table to start. It was a special event being with all three of her kids at once—a rare occasion. Scanning the dinner menu, she struggled to make a dinner decision.

"Boy, this is tough. The meat-and-cheese board sounds amazing and so does the baked brie. What do you think?"

Morgan brought her eyes up from the menu to find the oddest expressions on Brooklyn's and Ashley's faces. They were staring at something, eyes and mouth wide open.

"What's wrong with you guys?" Morgan asked, narrowing her eyes in question, while turning her head in the direction of their bulging eyeballs.

It didn't take long for the answer to emerge. Dylan was headed straight for them. Morgan turned back around, leaning toward the girls with her napkin.

"Let me just wipe the drool a bit before he gets here," she said.

"Morgan—hey!" Dylan said, leaning down to give her a big hug.

Brooklyn and Ashley looked dumbfounded. Justin set his menu down to check this guy out. Stroking his goatee, he looked Dylan up and down, assessing the intruder's appearance.

"Hi Dylan. What a nice surprise. Please sit down and join us," Morgan said.

He didn't hesitate and took a seat right next to Brooklyn.

Morgan felt a light tap on her shoulder. When she looked up to respond, Brody stood tall beside her, those sexy green eyes penetrating right into her soul.

"Brody—hi." She stood to embrace him.

She'd never seen him dressed up quite like this. Every piece was black with the exception of his silver chain that hung low. A soft black V-neck t-shirt, fresh-looking black jeans, and a light blazer rolled up at the sleeves, leaving his tattooed arms slightly exposed. He wore a large silver ring on his right hand that looked custom-made. Morgan glanced down at his shoes to find him wearing black Converse high tops.

"Please, sit down. I was just about to introduce everyone. Kids, this is my friend Brody Mason and his son Dylan. They have a home down the way from me."

She cleared her throat and continued.

"Actually, it's a rather funny story. I injured myself at the beach the first week I was here and Brody came to my rescue. I'm forever grateful." She smiled and looked at Brody with appreciation.

"Holy shit!" Justin blurted out, nearly jumping out of his seat. "You're members of Keyed Up!"

He leaned over the table to shake Brody's hand. "I can't believe this. You know our mom? I love your music."

Feeling a bit awkward for being recognized, Brody smiled and thanked Justin for his support.

Brooklyn hadn't taken her eyes off Dylan since he'd sat down. They chatted in their own corner, talking about music and her work. She'd moved to Venice Beach to do a tattoo internship. Between their edgy careers and personalities, they were hitting it off.

Ashley sat quietly, her eyes drifting back and forth from Morgan to Brody. Something had her curious about the two of them.

Justin continued to sit starstruck, asking Brody about the new album and concert tours.

"You guys should join us for dinner. Right, Mom?" Justin said.

"Um ... no pressure guys," Morgan said. "But yes, of course we would love that."

Brody brushed his leg up against the side of Morgan's. He was dying to touch her, among other things.

"We can stay. Sounds great," Dylan said and flashed a grin across the table.

Brody looked at Morgan and smiled. He could hear a ballad playing in the background and leaned in close to her ear.

"How about a dance, lover?" he whispered, causing a shiver to flutter down her neck.

"I'd love to," she whispered back.

Brody stood and took her hand to escort her to the dance floor. She didn't need eyes in the back of her head to know her kids were staring. She could feel the intense curiosity slapping her on the back. She hadn't been ready or prepared to explain Brody to them. Things had happened unexpectedly, and how on earth would she tell them she had a *lover*? The only man her kids had ever seen her with was Steven, their father.

On the dance floor, Brody held out his hand again for Morgan. She took it and stepped in, closing the distance between them. One hand held his and the other rested gently on his shoulder, as they began swaying to the Journey ballad.

"Morgan, I have no idea how to act around your kids. We've never discussed what to tell people. Do you want me to be discreet, or ...?" Brody felt perplexed.

"I know, Brody. I'm sorry. They've never seen me with a man other than their father. It's complicated. We obviously didn't see this whole thing coming."

"I don't do well with restrictions, sweetheart." Brody said.

He pulled her in closer, his hands rubbing up and down her bare back. His head moved into the crook of her neck. She could smell his cologne and closed her eyes to savor it. She pulled back to look into his eyes. She wanted his mouth on hers right now. Brody knew it was an invitation, and he didn't waste a second to oblige.

Dylan acted as if nothing strange were going on. He sat back nonchalantly, trying not to notice the shocked and quizzical looks on everyone's faces. Ashley was first to crack.

"What the hell is going on here, Dylan? Is your dad seducing my mom? I mean—oh my God—his tongue is down her throat right now!" Ashley rambled in distress.

Justin and Brooklyn looked at their sister and tried to hold back laughter.

Wearing a devilish grin, Dylan responded.

"Oh yeah. My dad has it *bad* for your mom. He tries to play it cool, but I can see right through him. They've been leading up to this ever since they met several weeks ago. I think it's great. Morgan is amazing."

Dylan narrowed his eyes at Ashley, taking in the look of utter shock on her face.

Justin spoke up. "Come on, Ashley. She was bound to start dating at some point. And how cool is it that she's seeing *Brody Mason* of all people?"

"Don't start with me, Justin. I think it would've been nice if Mom discussed this with us before we had to watch—*that* out *there*—in the middle of the dance floor, no less."

"Here they come," Dylan said. "Be cool everybody. Ashley, it's going to be all right. Shhh."

Brody and Morgan sat back down at the dinner table. Everyone sat quietly, the elephant in the room hovering. Morgan picked up her menu with one hand and tapped her fingers nervously on the table with her other. Her eyes flashed across the table to Ashley, who refilled her champagne flute all the way to the top.

"Oysters tonight. Most definitely!" Morgan announced.

Ashley's response was a violent projection of sparkling wine from her mouth followed by uncontrollable choking. Justin reached over to pat her back.

"Honey, are you all right?" Morgan asked, eyes narrowing with concern.

"Yes … mmhmm … fine, Mom …" Ashley said, trying desperately to breathe. She knew all too well that oysters were the classic aphrodisiac.

Observant enough to change the subject, Dylan interjected, bragging about the new album. It turned out to be a brilliant distraction, as Morgan's kids hung on every word.

"We're tying up loose ends right now, but we'll be ready for release very soon," he said.

"Brody, that's amazing. I know how hard you've all been working. Congratulations," Morgan said.

Her words came from the heart. Still, conflict stirred. Once the album was done, they'd part ways. Things had barely started between them. It would be over before she knew it. Could it be Brody was feeling the same turmoil?

Not likely, she thought.

* * *

Brody took the last bite of his steak, wiped his mouth, and tossed the napkin aside.

"Excuse me for a moment," he said and disappeared from the patio.

The mood at the table had lightened up, thanks to Dylan. There was a lull of silence from full, satisfied bellies.

"Oh man, I'm stuffed. What a great meal," Justin said.

Brody wandered back over and stood at Morgan's side, resting his hand on her shoulder.

"How about we all ride home together? I have a car waiting out front. We're all going to the same place, basically," he offered.

Brooklyn and Justin lit up like firecrackers, while Ashley played it cool.

"Looks like we're in, Brody. Thank you. But I need to take care of our check first." Morgan said.

"Already taken care of."

"What? Brody—no. I couldn't—"

"Stop, Morgan. Yes, you can. It's my pleasure. Let's go."

The whole crew piled into the black limousine, excitement overflowing. Justin and Brooklyn snapped selfies, and Dylan was gracious enough to agree to being in a few.

Brody looked at Morgan, "Is Ashley going to be okay? She's awfully quiet."

"Honestly, I don't know. She's very protective of me. I'm a little scared to go home, actually."

"Have fun with that, babe. Ha ha," he teased.

The limo pulled into Morgan's driveway. Dylan escorted her kids to the door while Brody and Morgan stayed back in the car to steal a moment alone.

"The kids are going home tomorrow. Thank you for everything tonight, Brody. We all had a wonderful evening."

Brody grabbed the back of her head to pull her in for a kiss. Their tongues locked, eager with need. Desire escalated as they groped each other.

The car door swung open and Morgan pulled back. Dylan's long leg shot through the door as he lowered his head to get in.

"Shit—goodnight, Morgan," Brody said, blowing out a breath of frustration.

"Goodnight, Brody."

Brody watched as she got out of the limo and disappeared into the small cottage.

As soon as she walked inside, her kids were ready to pounce.

Ashley was first to interrogate. "Mom. *You've* been holding out on us. How long has this been going on? Is it serious?"

Morgan looked over at Brooklyn, who sat casually on the sofa, legs crossed, and smiling amusedly. Justin leaned against the living-room wall, arms crossed over his chest.

"Look, you guys. It's a summer fling. No big deal. I'm sure it must be weird for you to think of me that way, but Brody and I agreed no strings, no commitments. Is that okay with everyone?" Morgan was annoyed at feeling like a scolded child.

"Seriously, Ashley. Put your claws back in," Justin said shaking his head.

He meant it to be funny, but Ashley sneered at her brother with a solid *fuck you* behind it. Brooklyn, who was always referred to as "the quiet one," continued to sit back, entertained by the scene at hand. It took a lot of effort to get Brooklyn to expose much of herself.

However, tonight Morgan was thankful for her hush-hush personality.

* * *

Morgan's love life had been taken off the table for the evening as everyone decided to turn in for bed. She felt agitated but not because Ashely had drilled her. Morgan knew her actions were based on love and concern. She felt incredibly lucky to have children who cared so much.

She climbed into bed only to toss and turn. All she could think about was Brody. Feeling spontaneous, she shot off her bed and changed into a tight-fitting summer dress. She peeked out her bedroom door to confirm that her kids were asleep.

I feel like a teenager trying to sneak out of the house.

The television had been left on, perfect for Morgan's escape plan. She tiptoed past the living room and slipped out the back patio door. Once her feet hit the sand, she took off running toward Brody's place.

Please, please let him still be awake, the voice inside her head begged.

The moon hovered just above Brody's deck, aiding as a glowing porch light for Morgan to find her way. She slowed her run to a stop and paused to catch her breath before she headed up the back stairway.

She found herself frozen to take the first step. Would Brody think this was too aggressive and intrusive?

Slowly easing her way up the stairs, Morgan called out his name in a low voice. "Brody ... you up there?" She tapped on the wooden banister to announce her presence.

"Morgan?"

She could hear his steps approaching as she reached the top of the stairs.

"Hey," she said, swaying nervously with her hands behind her back. "I know this might not be okay, but I had to see you, Brody," she confessed, terrified she was making a fool out of herself.

He swept her up into his arms and carried her into the house. He stopped short in the kitchen, put her down, and bent her over the butcher-block island. She could feel his breath on the back of her neck as he leaned in to kiss her. She stretched her arms across the island for support as Brody bent down to lift up the back of her sundress and peel off her lace panties. Breathing heavily, Morgan allowed it. His hand came up between her legs to caress her clit and she spread her legs for him.

"God, Morgan. You *are* ready."

She could hear his pants fall and anticipated his desire to make a swift entrance. He entered her slowly, gently moving in and out of her. One hand squeezed the top of her shoulder while the other gripped the side of her waist. Brody's thrusting became more intense. Harder, faster.

"Are you all right, sweetheart?" he asked, short of breath.

Morgan grabbed the side of the island with her hand for support and nodded.

One last thrust and Brody held tight to her as he came with force.

After taking a moment to recover, Brody tried to find the strength to pull his pants back up. His legs burned as he bent down to pick up Morgan's panties off the floor.

The moment Morgan stood he embraced her, pushing aside the tough persona he carried. They moved to his bedroom and continued to make love until their bodies gave out.

* * *

Light had begun to illuminate the room through the sliding-glass door, alerting Morgan that she needed to leave—and soon. Looking at the clock on the nightstand, Morgan was shocked at the time.

"Oh my God, Brody. I have to get home before my kids wake up." She rolled over to plant a kiss on his cheek.

Brody quickly maneuvered Morgan's body on top of his. His hands came up to run his fingers through her hair, coercing her head toward his so he could kiss her. Morgan could feel the arousal building.

"Brody—" she said, trying to come up for air. "I'd love to do this all day, but—"

"I know, I know. Your kids are leaving today and you don't want to get caught doing the walk of shame," he said and laughed.

"I never thought of it like that—but yeah." Morgan rolled off the bed, rummaging around the floor for her dress and undies.

"Hopefully I can get back in the house without getting caught. This is so ridiculous. I'm a grown-ass woman."

Brody sat up in bed with his arms behind his head for support, watching her scramble to get dressed. He found her predicament amusing.

"I gotta go." Morgan blew a kiss at Brody as she fled out the door.

* * *

Morgan devised a plan as she ran back to the cottage.

Maybe they never noticed I was gone.

She climbed the steps to the back deck slowly, one by one on tiptoe, head stretched out like an ostrich's to see if there were any signs of life.

So far so good.

She focused on being stealth, moving like a cougar to the sliding-glass door. Her hand gripped the handle and tugged ever so slightly.

"Mom—what are you doing?"

Morgan jumped backward. Ashley sat in a lounge chair positioned in the corner of the deck. She raised her coffee mug for a sip.

"Ashley! You scared the shit out of me. Oh my God—my heart. I can't breathe."

"Sorry … just wondering why you were tiptoeing and all. Long night?"

"Are Justin and Brooklyn awake too?" Morgan asked, ignoring Ashley's question.

"'fraid so. Don't worry. I've got your back. We'll just say you were out being neighborly," Ashley said flippantly.

Morgan walked over to take a seat next to Ashley.

"Look, honey. I'm truly sorry you had to find out about Brody this way. I feel bad that you're so upset. The thing is, I'm not doing anything wrong. Just be happy for me, please."

Ashley swung her legs around to look Morgan in the eye.

"If he hurts you, I will personally kick his rock 'n' roll ass."

"Yes, of course. He will be at the hand of your wrath," Morgan promised. "I love you, Ashley. You always look out for me and it never goes unnoticed."

Ashley hugged her and went back inside the cottage. Morgan's body fell back onto the lounge chair in relief. She thought of Steven and hoped he was happy she was trying to move on. Tears streamed down her face.

You will always be a part of me, Steven, and I will always be there for our kids.

CHAPTER NINE

BEHIND CLOSED DOORS

The summer was closing in on Morgan and her next move had yet to be decided.

Justin and Ashley had invited her to stay with them in Denver for a while. It was the most practical decision for the short term. She'd be able to focus on her photography—Colorado was filled with beautiful scenery. Foraging through her prints, Morgan was pleased with her inventory thus far, but she could use more inspiration and different landscapes. She'd never been interested in photographing people.

One particular photo of the tide pools brought her memories back to her first day in Santa Cruz. The day she'd met Brody on the beach. Twisting her ankle in circles, she smiled, remembering how embarrassed she'd been when he found her.

Morgan's attention drifted to the beautiful sunset out her window. She stepped away from the pile of pictures and headed for the hall closet to grab a white cotton jacket to wear over her blue tank top. Her cut-off jean shorts were fraying at the edges, looking a bit ragged, but to Morgan, that was beach life. She grabbed her tan fedora on her way out the door and placed it on her head, twisting the length of her brown hair into a messy bun that rested off to the right side.

All summer long, Morgan had hoped to find a sand dollar or pieces of sea glass. This was the perfect opportunity to fit in some beach combing.

As soon as her feet hit the sand, she journeyed out into the water just until the waves hit her ankles. Crouching, she ran her fingers through the water and raked the sand, catching a pile in her hands. Holding up her palm, she ran her fingertips through the sand to see what treasures had been left behind. Just a few tiny shells, smaller than the tip of her pinky finger. Her eyes searched the beach for more vulnerable areas where the low tide had exposed precious items and creatures.

A whistling sound off in the distance broke Morgan's concentration. Feeling annoyed at the intrusion, she turned to find the culprit. Her irritated stance dissipated when she saw Jaxon on the back of Brody's deck. His long lanky arms were flailing back and forth in the air.

"Hey, Morgan! Morgan, up here!" He whistled again.

He's such a goof. Morgan grinned so wide the corners of her mouth wanted to crack.

Nate and Johnny ran up beside Jaxon to join in.

"Morgan—check this out!" Jaxon's voice penetrated the sea air.

"Oh no. What are they up to?" Morgan said out loud. She couldn't help but feel suspicious.

Suddenly, her mouth fell open and her hands instantly covered her shocked expression. "Huh ... oh my gosh..." She blushed.

Jaxon, Nate, and Johnny had dropped their drawers and were mooning Morgan from Brody's deck—right there for the whole world to see. They were laughing in a frenzy. Jaxon bent down to pull his pants back up, then his tall skinny body jerked back to attention and he screamed down to her.

"Get your ass up here. We're celebrating. Hurry the fuck up."

Gathering her composure, she waved to Jaxon and nodded. Chuckling to herself, Morgan trekked the beach toward Brody's house. She was still trying to recover from seeing their bare butts, white as mayo no less.

"Those assholes," she whispered.

She found Brody waiting for her as she reached the top of the stairs. He was wearing blue jeans and a tight black thermal shirt that enveloped his physical features. His dark hair was an out-of-control sexy mess. She stepped in for a hug then pulled back slightly to speak.

"So, what are we celebrating this evening? Must be pretty damn good since my invitation consisted of exposure from your band mates."

Brody hesitated, looking down at the ground and stuffing his hands inside his pockets. It was nervous fidgeting, which usually meant bad news. Morgan could spot the body language anywhere.

"We finished the album this afternoon. Our work here is done. Now we head back to LA to finalize. Everyone is—no pun intended—keyed up and ready to celebrate."

He smiled at Morgan and waited for her response. The completion of the album meant they'd be going their separate ways.

"Wow, Brody! Congratulations, really. I'm so happy for you." She stepped into his arms for a hug.

Her mind swirled. She wanted desperately to be happy for Brody, but her heart ached at what was coming. She reined him in even closer, not wanting to let go. Her head pressed deep into his chest.

Morgan, do not cry. DO NOT CRY!

This day had been coming and she'd promised him no strings. No heavy. Bawling her eyes out would be considered heavy in a man's mind. She pulled back to stand on her tiptoes and kiss him.

"Oh come on, you guys. No more of that mushy mushy. It's time to party!" Jaxon said.

Brody swung his head around. "Fuck off, Jaxon."

"You seem to tell him that a lot, I noticed." Morgan said. She grabbed for his hand. "Come on. Let's go inside and celebrate with the others."

It didn't take long before Brody's house was flooded with friends and beautiful women. Dylan showed up with several boxes of pizza and spotted Morgan with a beer in her hand, swaying to the music in the background. He set down the boxes that had caused his arm to go numb and walked over to her, draping the good arm around her shoulder. He pulled her in for a squeeze and kissed the top of her head.

She looked up his six-foot-something frame until she met his eyes and smiled. His endearing gesture spoke to Morgan: *I know what you're feeling, and I feel it, too.* She wrapped her arms around Dylan's waist and held on.

Brody had been on the other side of the room, resting against the wall, trying to considerately listen to a chatty blonde go on and on about absolutely nothing. He had to fight the urge to roll his eyes. Her voice had been in his ear for the last ten minutes, but his eyes were on Morgan the whole time. The giggling bombshell was clueless to the fact that he was somewhere else. She fluffed her big hair and adjusted her hot-pink push-up bra whose sole purpose was to catch Brody's eye. Before Morgan came along, he would've fallen for the flirtation and fucked the poor bitch in the bathroom by now.

He rubbed his hand over his face as reality hit him like a heavy blow to the abdomen. Morgan had gotten to him—both physically and emotionally. In an agitated movement, he pushed away from the wall and stormed off, leaving the woman behind to sulk.

Weaving his way in and out of the maze of people throughout the house and out to the back deck, Brody tried to make his way to Morgan. He spotted her tan fedora bouncing as she took the steps back down to the beach.

Shit—is she leaving?

He got his ass in gear, picking up the pace to catch up to her.

"Hey! Morgan—wait," he called out.

He tossed his beer bottle in the trash and ran toward Morgan. She turned around at the sound of his voice and watched him come toward her.

He stopped to stand right in front of her and reached out to grab the sides of her arms in an attempt to keep her from moving any further.

"What's going on? Are you leaving?" He stared down at her accusingly.

"I just needed to come out for some air. I was contemplating going home—but hopefully not alone, Brody."

Relief coursed through him, causing his body to relax. Her blunt invitation pleased him and he picked up her hand to lead the way to the cottage. They walked in silence, feeling the sea breeze brush across their faces.

Morgan dropped Brody's hand and took a few steps ahead of him, peeling her clothes off piece by piece in the process. The sun had gone down, leaving a sliver of moonlight. She turned to face him while her feet stepped backward, guiding them to the water.

"Join me?"

Brody's clothes were off within seconds as they both plunged into the ocean. When they emerged to the surface, Morgan swam to Brody and thrust her arms and legs around him. There was something that felt so damn good about two naked bodies rubbing up against each other in the water.

His mouth came down on hers forcefully and their tongues began to devour one another. The buoyancy from the water kept their bodies from sinking like an anchor. Goose bumps ran up and down her arms and she began to shiver.

"You're cold, babe. Let's go inside," Brody insisted.

Hesitant to let go, she agreed and they swam back to shore. Her arms wrapped around her exposed wet body as the frigid air attacked. Teeth chattering, she moved swiftly to locate her clothes that she'd strewn here and there. She felt her body become paralyzed at the sight of Brody's naked backside. Suddenly, finding her own clothes had become an afterthought as she took in the male revue right in front of her. Brody's blue jeans and bare torso seduced her like a snake charmer. She heard a faint voice trying to break her trance.

"Morgan?"

Shaking her head to encourage bodily function, Morgan realized Brody was looking at her with an amused grin. *Shit*. He'd discovered her gawking. Feeling like a kid with her hand caught in the cookie jar, Morgan blushed and continued fumbling around for her clothes.

Carrying the fedora in her hand, she led Brody to the back door of her cottage. He stepped inside first, taking her hand and leading her straight to the bathroom. No words were spoken as he pulled aside the floral shower curtain and turned the water on.

Steam began to rise, filling the small room with a cloud. Brody began to undress Morgan, removing each garment slowly and seductively. She stepped into the shower stall and grabbed a sponge to moisten soap. Brody's hand came around her stomach, signaling his arrival. His head came down to locate the side of her neck, imprinting erotic kisses over each drop of water glistening on her skin. She closed her eyes and relaxed to allow herself the pleasure.

After a few moments had passed, she turned around to face him, lifting the soapy sponge to the top of his chest. She began massaging in circular motions, while the suds left a slippery layer behind. Both hands were working and had manipulated their way right down his torso, where she stopped short.

Brody's erection presented itself to Morgan as an invitation. She put her mouth over his shaft and moved up and down, creating friction and pleasure. He gasped and held on to the back of her head. His breathing began to elevate and Morgan could feel his legs tense with anticipation.

"Fuck, babe—what are you doing to me? Oh fuck ...," he said in a gruff tone. She could feel his erection begin to pulse. One of his hands cupped the back of her head while the other held onto the side of the shower stall.

Morgan waited patiently while Brody recovered, not wanting to rush his enjoyment. She took the sponge and began scrubbing his legs, making sure not to miss a spot.

Brody reached down to pull her up and planted his mouth on hers forcefully. His arms came around her and held her tight. Water bounced like rain off their bodies and seeped into their mouths. They were drinking from one another and couldn't hydrate enough.

Brody turned things down a notch to shut off the water and step out of the shower. He grabbed a bath towel and held it up for Morgan to step into.

They moved into the bedroom and collapsed into bed. The passion and hot steam had left them in a state of exhaustion. Brody settled in behind Morgan and wrapped his arm around her. The air in the room was silent, yet heavy with unspoken words.

"Morgan. we're closing up the house and leaving for LA tomorrow. What are your plans? I mean, where will you be going when your lease is up?"

She nestled in closer, tightening her arms around his in fear he might let go. The turmoil inside her left her feeling irritated. She was angry for allowing herself to fall for this man.

"Morgan?" Brody pressed.

Clearing the emotion inside her, she responded.

"I'm going to Denver to live with Justin and Ashley for a while. I'm not ready to commit to my forever place, yet. I need ... more time."

Brody hesitated to respond while he reflected on her plans and the situation in front of them. The frog in his throat felt lodged, prohibiting him from speaking what was in his heart. Choosing the Band-Aid approach—not the one where you just rip it off, but the one where you simply cover things up—Brody sealed his emotions, ignoring what would fester underneath.

"That's a good plan, Morgan. You can continue your work and enjoy the company of your kids."

"Yeah ... that's exactly what I thought. It's for the best right now." She was trying to sway the conversation to a close.

The more they talked the harder it would be to stay strong. Morgan begged for sleep to take over and rescue her. The morning would raise its ugly head soon enough, and she needed the stamina to say goodbye to Brody.

* * *

Morgan woke up to find Brody sitting in the chair beside her bed. His arms were folded across his chest and it seemed his thoughts were out to sea.

"Good morning," she said as she stretched and yawned.

Brody walked over to kneel in front of her before she could get out of bed. His arm came out and began stroking the side of her head.

"Don't get up, sweetheart. I have to go. Just stay in bed and try to get more sleep."

Her body bolted upward. "What? Wait—no, Brody."

She tried pulling the covers off her legs to leave the bed, but his hands blocked them. He was looking at her so seriously, so adamantly.

"Brody—"

Morgan's hurt voice pulled at his heart.

He swallowed the lump in his throat to speak. "I have to walk away now, Morgan. This is the only way I can do it. Please understand. You deserve better than this, I know. I just ... I'm a fucking asshole, Morgan, and you're better off without me."

The tears began streaming down Morgan's cheeks and she didn't even realize it. His lips came down on hers softly, gently.

"Goodbye, Morgan," he whispered as he slowly stood to turn and walk away.

Morgan sat there troubled at what had just happened. This wasn't the way she'd envisioned saying goodbye. She clenched the bedsheets tightly against her bare chest and watched Brody leave. For good.

CHAPTER TEN

WALKING ON PINS AND NEEDLES

"Jaxon! Make sure all the windows and doors are locked. Once we leave, I'm not coming back here," Brody said.

The band had spent the entire day trying to button down the Santa Cruz house for the next several months.

"I want to leave today. No matter what," he said.

"Damn—someone's brooding today," Jaxon said under his breath.

Brody stepped out into the driveway to toss his belongings into the limousine waiting to take them to LA.

"I think this is the last of it," Dylan said, pausing to observe his dad's grumpy demeanor. "Dad, are you all right? You've been … kind of a dick today."

Brody ignored the question and threw on his black aviator sunglasses.

"Round up the guys and let's get the fuck out of here," he said, bending down to step inside the limo.

Dylan stood with his hands on his hips while Brody's back told him to mind his own fucking business. Dylan turned to go back inside the house, dreading the drive home.

"I was going to leave the Escalade here, but maybe I shouldn't. Dad's unbearable today," Dylan said looking at Jaxon.

"Yeah—no shit. It's going to be a long ride home," Jaxon said, dragging his heels.

"Dylan, you can't bail on us, man. If we have to endure it, so do you," Nate said.

"All right then, let's rock 'n' roll," Dylan said, locking the door behind them as they left.

The limo drove off, inevitably passing Morgan's cottage. Brody could feel all eyes on him. He had his head buried in paperwork, trying to appear distracted. There was no in hell he was going to look up at them and surrender his vulnerability.

"Dylan, once we get back to LA we have a lot to do. I want to get the ball rolling on the concert tour dates and venues. *Behind Closed Doors* needs to be ready to launch by September first," he said.

"I'm on it," Dylan reassured him.

* * *

Once the band arrived in LA, the traffic was predictably horrific. Cars were moving in a stop-and-go formation, while others honked annoyingly as if that would actually make a difference.

"And that would be the sound of home, along with the layer of smog hovering like a black cloud," Jaxon said, trying to lighten up the mood.

"Home sweet home," Johnny interjected.

They dropped Brody and Dylan off first. As soon as Brody stepped out of the car, he could feel the difference in the air. The sun's rays penetrated right through him, creating beads of sweat on his forehead. His tall frame turned from one direction to the other, trying to find the sea breeze he'd been accustomed to in Santa Cruz.

"God, it's Africa hot today," Dylan complained.

They took their belongings into the house and headed straight for the air-conditioning thermostat.

"Dad, I'm going on home. I have things to get caught up on. We can head over to the recording studio first thing in the morning." Dylan reached out to shake his dad's hand.

Brody pulled him in for a hug.

"Thanks, man. I appreciate all your hard work. This album is going to kick ass!"

He walked Dylan to his red Dodge Challenger and waved him off, feeling relieved to finally be alone. Brody didn't do well around people when something was eating away at him.

He walked back into the house, pausing to look around and familiarize himself. The atmosphere was dead quiet and there was a musty smell stuck in the air from the house being closed up all summer. He walked over to the refrigerator to find it fully stocked with his favorite beer and a few groceries. Reaching inside, he grabbed a cold one and made a mental note to thank his housekeeper.

He found some shade in the backyard and sat down, one leg crossed over the other. The first sip of beer was always the best. Crisp and cold, with the carbonation exploding in the back of his throat. The bottle was sweating cold dew, encouraging Brody to hold it up to his flushed cheeks and forehead. He'd forced himself not to think of Morgan, but he caved when the effects of the beer began to settle in.

The temper inside him began to build. He stood and threw the bottle, watching it shatter against the bricks of the privacy fence.

"Fuck!" Brody said, rubbing his hands over his face.

He buried himself in work, forcing himself to go to bed around two a.m. It seemed like a flash of a moment before he was awakened by the banging from the front door.

* * *

"Yo, Dad. Time to get moving." Dylan's voice traveled. He'd let himself in and waited patiently in the kitchen for Brody to arrive.

Dylan was determined there'd be no poking the bear today. He was leaning up against the kitchen counter, foot tapping nervously, when Brody walked in.

"Hey—I brought some coffee." Dylan handed him the steaming cup of joe.

Brody took off the lid, breathing in the scent and allowing it to cool.

"You don't look so good, Dad," Dylan said, concerned.

Brody gave him an irritable glance. "I was up until two a.m. and I'm not a fucking teenager anymore," he growled.

What was that about not poking the bear?

"Right ... well, let's roll out, then. We can go over stuff in the car." He gestured for Brody to head outside.

It's going to be another one of those days. Dylan rolled his eyes and blew out a long breath.

* * *

The week seemed to drag on as the band wrapped up the album. The only thing the guys had seen was the inside of the recording studio. Brody had been consumed with what he did best: work. Music was his passion, his utter focus.

"This is it, guys. We're scheduled for some interviews next week and then *Behind Closed Doors* comes to life. Take the weekend to rest, have fun, or whatever because starting next week, we won't have time to shit," Brody warned.

"Brody, why don't we go hit up Sunset Strip? We haven't done that in a while. Let's turn things up." Jaxon said.

Brody knew what Jaxon was up to. He'd never get back to his old self if he didn't saddle up and fuck some meaningless women.

"I'm heading home and staying in. There are some loose ends I need to tie up, but by all means, go knock yourself out. I'm sure Nate and Johnny will be happy to join. Dylan, can you come by on Saturday for a few hours to work and then we can kick back?"

Dylan cleared his throat, pausing awkwardly before responding.

"Actually, Dad ... I'm heading up to Venice Beach for the weekend. Brooklyn invited me to come hang out and see where she works. Should be fun. Did I mention we've been talking since she left Santa Cruz?"

Brody's eyes squinted at Dylan as he processed what had just been said. He reached up to stroke his chin, feeling the prickliness of his beard stubble.

Jaxon broke the silence, walking up to Dylan and slapping him on the back.

"You sneaky son of a bitch. You've been holding out on us. This is so bad ass. Give us details."

"Just hold on one damn minute," Brody said. "This is Morgan's daughter you're talking about, Jaxon. I don't *want* to hear any details. Not the kind I'm sure your perverted ass wants to hear."

Jaxon was laughing inside. It was cruel, he knew, but he loved getting his buddy all riled up.

"Dad, you're cool with this, right?" Dylan asked, hoping for his approval. Nate, Johnny, and Jaxon took that as a queue to leave and give them space to hash things out.

"We're out, Brody. Get yourself laid or something this weekend, for God's sake." Jaxon said.

Nate and Johnny followed, smiling at Brody in a smart-ass way. The door slammed behind them and Dylan prepared himself for his dad's response.

Brody began to pace the room, then turned to face Dylan.

"Just … be careful, Dylan. She seems like a strong, confident girl, but our career makes it nearly impossible to have relationships. You know—the committed, long-lasting kind. Brooklyn needs to be fully aware of what she's getting herself into." His tone sounded desperate.

"I've got this, Dad. Brooklyn and I have a lot in common. We're taking things slow, just getting to know each other."

"All right then. It's your business anyway. Has she mentioned Morgan at all? How is she?"

"Morgan packed up and left Santa Cruz a few days after us. She's in Denver now with Justin and Ashley. Dad, why don't you just call her? I know you care about her and there's nothing wrong with that. You can be so stubborn. From what Brooklyn says, Morgan's quiet and shut-off. I think both of you need to stop this nonsense and embrace your feelings for one another. Dad, you haven't been serious with anyone since Mom, and that was a long fucking time ago."

"Morgan and I agreed not to get into the heavy, Dylan. I'm about to go on the road. It wouldn't be right and that's just the end of it, all right?"

Dylan threw his hands up.

"All right, all right. I've got to go, Dad. Try to have a good weekend. If you aren't going to allow yourself to love and receive love, then I agree with Jaxon. Get drunk, get laid, and snap out of this grumpy attitude you've got going on. It sucks for all of us."

With that, Dylan turned and walked out the door. He felt like a disrespectful asshole for talking to his dad that way, but he couldn't handle his sulking anymore.

It was a hard pill to swallow, but Brody knew Dylan was right. "Shit!" he burst out, kicking the music stand in front of him and sending it crashing to the ground.

CHAPTER ELEVEN

MOVING BEYOND THE SETBACKS

Morgan stepped out onto the back deck of the Denver home she thankfully shared with Ashley and Justin. A drift of crisp air touched her senses as an image of early fall emerged. The aspen trees were bright green, shedding a single leaf on and off throughout the day. Justin had spent hours all summer keeping the lawn alive.

Morgan kicked off her sandals and gracefully walked down the patio stairs to step onto the cool grass. Her stride was slow, her face never looking away from the velvety texture beneath her.

As the sun began to go down, she felt a chill and wrapped her arms protectively around her shoulders. Justin had come home from work and was watching his mom from the kitchen window. A sadness came over him, as he infringed upon her private moment. He could feel his mom's pain and wanted desperately to stop it. He opened the back door to greet her.

"Hey, Mom! Ashley's working at the brewery tonight. What do you say we head down there for dinner?"

He'd caught her off guard and she spun around.

"Justin—hey. I didn't even hear you come home. You startled me a bit." She laughed at herself.

She walked toward him, pausing to rest her foot on the first step of the stairs to the deck.

"Let me go change. Getting out of the house sounds great," she said.

Justin smiled and took her hand, pulling her to meet him at the top. They both retreated to their bedrooms to change and freshen up.

Morgan rummaged through her closet, realizing she hadn't finished unpacking since arriving in Denver. It wasn't like her to be lazy and unmotivated. She bent down and picked up her duffle bag, emptying the remaining items on the closet floor. Fishing through the messy pile, Morgan picked out a pair of jean leggings and began pulling them over her legs. She extracted a white long-sleeved t-shirt from a hanger and threw it over her head, exposing one bare shoulder. Her favorite blue suede boots called to her from the corner of her eye. She grabbed them from the shelf and began slipping in one foot at a time, careful not to catch her leggings in the zipper. She fluffed her soft brown hair and took one glance into the full-length mirror on her way out of the room.

Justin sat on the beige sofa, legs crossed, scrolling through his smartphone while he waited.

"Okay, let's do this thing. I'm ready to go," Morgan said.

He looked up from his phone and smiled. One of the things that Justin admired about his mom was that she always made an effort to look nice. Lately, however, she hadn't been herself and it had caught his attention.

"You look amazing, Mom." Justin said, as he stood and escorted her out the front door.

* * *

Ashley was a server at a craft brewery near downtown Denver. It was a two-story building with a rooftop seating area that had panoramic views of downtown. The hostess seated Justin and Morgan in one of Ashley's sections at a high-top table on the patio. Music burst through the surround-sound speakers and there were large TV screens mounted in several corners of the patio. Morgan's body moved to the music as she began to scan the room. Happy hour was in full swing, as well as all the people-watching that came with it.

Ashley walked toward their table, waving in acknowledgment. She took a seat right next to Justin, expressing the need to take a load off. Blowing out a long breath, Ashley started in.

"I swear, if one more person asks me if there are onions in the tuna salad, I'm going to lose it. It's right there on the menu. And, by the way, apparently there's a sign on my back that says *grab my ass.*"

Justin choked on his beer, laughing at his sister's predicament. Ashley slapped the side of his arm.

"It's not funny, Justin. How would you like to be groped all day long? Never mind—don't answer that question."

Morgan grinned, amused at the banter between them. The dark cloud over Ashley's head was soon diminished by Justin's heckling. She continued her nonstop chatter while she took their order, then moved on to her next victims.

"I seriously would *not* want to be the one on the other end of the hand that grabs Ashley's rear end. Can you imagine? The hellcat she is? Poor schmuck." Justin shook his head.

"For sure. Brooklyn and Ashley can both hold their own. That's why they never got bullied growing up." Morgan lifted her beer for a quick swig.

Something had caught the corner of her eye from the big-screen TV behind the bar. Her eyebrows furrowed as she focused to get a better look. She stood from her stool to walk over to the bar.

"Mom?" Justin watched her walk away in a trance. His eyes never left her as he wondered what the hell was going on. She was fixated on the TV in front of her.

"Oh no—shit," he said under his breath.

Brody was larger than life right there on every TV screen on the patio. He was being interviewed, along with the rest of the band. Justin walked up behind his mom and rested his hand gently on her shoulder.

"Mom..." He spoke softly.

"Looks like *Behind Closed Doors* is about to be released," Morgan said, a slight smile surfacing.

Her heart was pounding so hard it felt like it could leap out of her chest. Her hand came up to touch the top of Justin's, acknowledging his protectiveness. Seeing Brody had stirred up every emotion possible.

"Hey, how about we have Ashley pack up our food to go," Justin said. "I'll get the fire pit going and we can just chill out back."

Morgan nodded and turned to grab her purse off the table.

"I'll wait in the car, okay?"

Her pace was brisk, as she vacated the restaurant, hoping the tears that threatened to burst would hold off a while longer. She got into Justin's blue Lexus, shut the door, and allowed the dams to open. Her cell phone chimed as an incoming text turned up. She picked up the phone and saw it was from Ashley.

I love you, Mom.

Morgan sobbed even harder.

She saw Justin approaching the car and worked quickly to wipe the evidence of her tears away. Peeking in the rearview mirror, she found red bulging eyes and flaming cheeks.

'Crap. I'm the image of a heartbroken teenager. I'm too old for this shit," she said out loud.

Justin climbed in, threw their dinner in the back seat, and sped out of the parking lot. He opened the sun roof to persuade the fresh Colorado air to filter in. Morgan closed her eyes, welcoming the breeze to sashay through her strands of hair. Her skin began to cool down from the irritation the tears had left behind. She opened her eyes and was struck by the thousands of stars in the sky looking down at her. "So beautiful," she said, a bit uplifted.

Justin looked over at her and smiled. "Everything's going to be okay, Mom. I promise."

* * *

The next day, Morgan slept later than usual. The sun had been up for hours, shedding light into her bedroom in an effort to promote movement and energy. She pulled the sheets over her head, grunting at the idea of facing the day. She hadn't accomplished anything since arriving to Denver. Her camera had sat lonely, just waiting for her to get busy. The few prints she'd brought to Denver with her were collecting dust, forgotten on the oak desk in her room.

A light tapping sound came from her bedroom door, followed by a creaking that alerted her someone was opening it.

"Mom? Are you up yet?" Ashley hesitantly poked her head inside. Morgan pulled the covers back down and smiled at her concerned daughter.

"Yep. Just mapping out my day in my head before I jump into the shower. I have a lot to get done." She felt guilty for stretching the truth. She hadn't thought about actually getting up at all.

Ashley walked over to the desk and picked up one of the photos. She held it up for a closer look and blew the dust off it, turning to look at Morgan with one eyebrow raised quizzically. She picked up a few more and studied them.

"Mom, these are really good. What are your plans? You are going to sell them, right? Look at how you captured Brody in this one as if you weren't even trying."

Morgan flew out of the bed and grabbed the photo out of Ashley's hand.

"What are you talking about? I didn't take any shots of Brody ... ever." She examined the photo closely. At first glance, the image was of the sunset hovering over the ocean.

"Look *here*, Mom," Ashley instructed, using her index finger to point out the obvious.

"How could you miss it? It tells a story. This man, watching down on something or someone. What is he looking at? What is he thinking? It's pretty fucking mysterious. Way to go, Mom."

"I had no idea I'd captured his house on the cliffs. That *is* him, standing there looking out the window."

She felt short of breath at the sight of him. Instantly inspired, she picked up the rest of the photos, inspecting each one closely.

"I'll leave you to it, Mom. I have to go to work. This is just the tip of the iceberg, you know? You have dozens of photos in that camera just waiting to be born. Do your thing." Ashley said, closing the door behind her as she walked out.

Morgan had always intended to sell her photos and had devoted much time over the summer trying to come up with ideas on how to make them uniquely her own and desirable to others. She was angry at herself for losing focus and getting off track. She'd fallen into a depression and it was time to either suck it up or change the situation at hand.

Suddenly, a wild idea emerged. Picking up her cell phone, she dialed Brooklyn.

This is crazy, but what the hell ...

CHAPTER TWELVE

THE CRAZY THINGS WOMEN DO

Flashing lights. Thumping bass drum. Screaming fans with their hands pounding upward into the air. Keyed Up had a sold out show in LA kicking off the *Behind Closed Doors* tour.

A murmuring chant began to fill the arena as Jaxon teased the crowd from his throne. The anticipation was building to a height of maximum overload. Dylan watched from the control center, making sure lights and sound were in proper working order. He gave Brody the thumbs up to take the stage and the rest of the band followed. Nate grabbed the mic and the ground floor of people shoved and crowded closer to the stage.

The rush and thrill hit Brody like lightning and he fucking loved it. He looked out across the arena and was overwhelmed by the number of bodies moving in rhythm to the music, singing along with every song. Witnessing the enthusiasm among the crowd amplified the satisfaction Brody felt, confirming that without a doubt, being a musician was his calling.

The two-hour performance had flown by as Keyed Up wrapped up the final set. Stepping down from his drum kit, Jaxon joined the rest of the band at the front of the stage to take a bow and wave the fans goodbye. Women pushed and squeezed through others to get closer, reaching their hands, begging to be noticed and invited backstage. Jaxon was a sucker for the beautiful ladies and bent down to touch their hands.

Nate led the posse through a dark dungeon path with long, narrow hallways, winding one way and then another. A room specifically for the band awaited their arrival. Brody's stance was his typical cool, low-key swagger. The rest of the band picked up the pace as they got closer—they knew what was waiting behind closed doors. There would be hot women, booze, and an enormous amount of food. The key essentials to an after-party. Jaxon was first to step inside.

"Oh, how I've missed this," he said as he took in the room.

No frills: just a true man cave with a nasty brown leather sectional sofa, a fully stocked bar, and a fifty-two-inch TV, blasting rock 'n' roll off Pandora. Nate was hit with an intense whiff of strong perfume and it hypnotized him to follow the scent. A smile surfaced when he discovered several women lingering, looking like they'd come straight from a ZZ Top video. Big hair, black fishnet stockings, and stilettos so high they could injure someone. The room screamed sex.

Dylan had beat them to the room and was hovering around the bar, whiskey neat in hand. He poured two fingers for Brody and handed it to him.

"You guys kicked ass tonight. Not a bad way to start off a tour, Dad." Dylan clicked his glass against Brody's in celebration.

They slammed the whiskey and Dylan poured them each another.

"Oh boy. Look out Dad. A redheaded temptress headed straight for you."

Brody stiffened as he sensed someone standing right behind him, arms gently wrapping around his torso.

"Hey Brody," the redhead whispered seductively in his right ear. She was wearing a tight black miniskirt and a white blouse tied at her midriff, exposing just enough skin to entice. Her legs were covered with black thigh-high boots that settled in between Brody's as she moved in closer behind him. He could feel her breasts against his back as her arms maneuvered around his waist. Acting unresponsive, Brody stood there, staring into his golden tonic, ready to throw it back any second.

Brody noticed that Dylan had been preoccupied and not the least bit interested in rescuing his dad from the situation at hand. Dylan lit up like a firecracker and headed for the doorway.

Brooklyn stood front and center looking exotic, with her long dark hair and crystal blue eyes. She had on blue jeans, black bootie high heels and a *Behind Closed Doors* concert t-shirt from the tour. The second Dylan reached her, they stepped into each other's embrace. Pulling back for a moment, Brooklyn had a concerned look on her face, as she observed the redhead groping Brody.

"Dylan, my Mom is here. She's going to walk in any moment."

His expression fell as he turned to look at Brody.

What the fuck is wrong with that woman? He obviously isn't interested, but it doesn't phase her one bit.

He turned to make his way to Brody to warn him but it was too late. Morgan had walked in and was standing under the doorway, eyes locked on Brody. Nausea and embarrassment flooded her body. Jaxon spotted her and yelled out.

"Morgan? Hey ..." His voice trailed off as he realized her expression was not a pleasant one. Brody heard her name and turned to figure out what the hell was going on, shoving the aggressive redhead to the side to get by her.

"Brody—what the fuck, you asshole," she whined as she tripped, nearly falling.

Brody's eyes found Morgan's, the look on her face mortified. She turned to run out of the room the second he saw her. Brody took off after her, following the sound of her shoes clicking on the concrete. She was wearing a tight-fitting white dress with a short blue jean jacket and sandals bearing a small heel, making it difficult to move quickly.

"Morgan! Morgan—please stop!" Brody yelled out.

She slowed down and eventually stopped, pausing to find the nerve to turn around and look at him. He caught up to her and approached cautiously.

"Morgan ... that wasn't what it—"

Morgan interrupted him.

"Brody, don't! You have nothing to explain. I ... I'm just a stupid woman thinking I'd just show up here to surprise you. I should've known better."

Tears began pooling in Morgan's eyes without her consent and it frustrated her. She looked down at the ground in embarrassment as Brody moved in closer. He reached out to touch her arm.

"Morgan, I'm so fucking happy to see you. Shocked, yes, but happy."

Her face came up to meet his. He reached up to wipe the tear falling down the side of her cheek.

Jaxon, Nate, and Johnny had piled around the doorway, stretching their heads as far as they could to see what Morgan would do.

"Shit—Morgan's pissed. I bet she turns around and slaps him good," Jaxon said, shaking his head.

"No way, Jaxon. Morgan has too much class for that. Oh no— she's crying. Goddammit Brody. His stubborn ass will ruin the best thing that ever happened to him," Johnny said.

Brooklyn was pacing back and forth inside the man cave wondering what was going on.

"You guys, get your nosey asses back inside here. They don't need you gawking and spying," she demanded, annoyed.

Dylan walked up to her and rubbed the sides of her shoulders.

"I know it looked real bad, but I'm telling you my dad wanted nothing to do with that chick or any others for that matter."

Brooklyn looked over at the women hovering around for attention. She folded her arms and gave them a glare that no one would want to endure.

"Why are they even here, Dylan? I mean, who invites them in anyway?" Brooklyn asked, anger building.

"Hey—they're just groupies. That kind of thing still exists. It's part of what goes along with what we do."

"Oh really? You can't just have foosball, Dungeons and Dragons ... shit like that guys love? Saying no to letting them in isn't allowed or something? Whatever, Dylan."

"Hey! Back off, Brooklyn."

He was attracted to her strong attitude and "don't fuck with me" confidence, but being the one she was mad at wasn't fun.

"Dylan, I can handle it. It's my mom I'm worried about. She hasn't been herself since she left Santa Cruz. I shouldn't have agreed to bring her here. I just fed her to the fucking wolves." Brooklyn raised her hand to her forehead in distress.

Dylan wrapped his arms around her and held her tight, kissing the top of her head.

* * *

Brody ran his fingers through Morgan's hair and bent down to kiss her. He started off light and gentle, barely touching her lips. Once he tasted her, it was all over. Both hands cradled her head as he took her mouth forcefully with need. She grabbed his t-shirt and held on as their tongues devoured each other. She stood on her tiptoes to get closer, moving her arms up around his neck.

"Yeah!" Jaxon blurted out, one arm punching the air. His eyes bugged out in surprise when he realized he'd just blown their cover. "Go, go, go ... back inside ... quick," he ordered the band.

They looked like roaches scurrying from a dark room when the lights were turned on.

"Shit—did they see us?" Nate asked, laughing uncontrollably.

"They're coming. Look busy ... act natural ... whatever the fuck you're supposed to be doing," Jaxon said.

He walked over to one of the ZZ Top girls and led her to the brown sofa where she plopped down onto his lap. Brooklyn shifted nervously, waiting for her mom to enter the room.

"I think we've had an audience," Brody said. "Come on, let's go join everyone. I know Jaxon is dying to see you."

He grabbed Morgan's hand to escort her to the man cave. She stopped just short of the door.

"Brody, I can't go in there. Those women—I just don't want to be around them."

"All right—no problem. Let's go to the tour bus, then. Give me one second, okay babe?" Brody asked, kissing her on the side of the cheek.

"Wait—Brody. Can you send Brooklyn out? I just want to make sure she's set for the evening."

Brody paused, looking at her with a concerned expression.

"Morgan, are you aware that Dylan and Brooklyn are ... well, let's just say ... getting to know one another?" He raised one eyebrow,

"I've been connecting the dots, but thank you for making me aware, Brody."

"I'll be right back. I need to straighten out a few things before we go. Just—*be here* when I get back, Morgan." He hesitated to leave her alone in the hallway.

"Brody! Where's my mom? Did she leave? Crap—"

"Calm down, Brooklyn. She's right out there waiting to talk to you. Everything's fine, I promise."

Brooklyn bolted out the door to find Morgan.

"Dylan, can you be sure to escort Brooklyn wherever she needs to be this evening? I'm taking Morgan back to the tour bus. I'm trying to throw something last-minute together." He picked up his cell phone to make a call, focused on Dylan's response.

"Our plan is to head back to Venice Beach. I'll meet up with you guys in San Francisco for the next show. I was just about to go make sure the set was disassembled and secured," Dylan said.

He walked over to Brody and slapped him on the back.

"Don't fuck this up, Dad," he said turning to walk out of the room.

Brody frowned at Dylan's back the whole way out the door. His words were lingering in Brody's mind. He was happy to see Morgan, but nothing had changed. The band was on tour and she saw firsthand this evening the reality of it all. Groupies coming and going, late nights and after-parties. It came with the territory.

Right now, all Brody wanted to do was enjoy the rest of the evening with Morgan. He had to live his life in the moment and was particularly excited about this one.

"Go on home, Brooklyn. I'm fine here, really. Enjoy the rest of your evening with Dylan. I'll text you tomorrow when I land in Denver," Morgan insisted, hugging her daughter goodnight.

Dylan walked up to take Brooklyn's hand and leave. She was hesitant, looking into her Mom's eyes with concern and uncertainty. Dylan's hand touched her back with a gentle push, coercing her to move.

"Call me if you need anything, Mom. I love you," Brooklyn said, turning to follow Dylan.

Morgan waved them off and found herself alone in the corridor. She folded her arms and paced back and forth until Brody finally showed up.

"I can't believe you're here, Morgan. Come on—I'm famished and we have a lot of catching up to do."

He took Morgan's hand and locked his fingers inside hers as they walked the quiet abandoned passage.

Brody stopped to push open a heavy door releasing them from the dark tunnel. The light from the full moon glowed, while the mild LA temperature welcomed their arrival outdoors. Morgan looked around to find them standing in an empty secluded parking lot outside the arena. Off in the distance was a home on wheels, also known as the tour bus for Keyed Up. As they approached, a tall man was waiting to greet them. He stood about six five with bulging muscles and gray hair that complimented his tough persona.

"Morgan, this is Frank, our security guard. He also drives the tour bus. We'd be lost without him."

Morgan was caught off guard when Frank reached out to shake her hand and a beautiful white smile surfaced on his intimidating face. She felt herself soften and found Frank endearing. He stepped aside to pull the curtain open on Brody's plans for the evening.

The first thing that caught Morgan's eye were the white lights dangling from the awning of the bus. Underneath sat a small table with a mason jar sitting in the center, a candle glowing inside. Two wine glasses sat empty, just waiting to be filled.

"Oh my gosh. Look at all of this. It's so beautiful. Brody … how? When?"

He slapped Frank's arm and said, "It was all Frank. I just made the call."

Frank smiled at Brody and headed inside the tour bus to leave them alone.

"Don't get too excited. We ordered pizza. Not very romantic, but quick and easy," Brody said, showing Morgan to her seat.

He sat down across from her and picked up a bottle of red wine, looking around the table for the wine opener.

"Here we go. Nothing like a little Two Buck Chuck to impress a lady," Brody teased as he filled Morgan's glass.

Little did he know that back in the day, Morgan had drunk her fair share of the inexpensive wine, finding it completely palatable. Cheap wine, expensive wine—it didn't matter. Morgan was happy sharing this time with him and would drink anything and love it. They clicked glasses and sipped the dark burgundy liquid.

"Oh shit—" Brody coughed, covering his mouth. "This really sucks. Jack Daniel's is smoother than this turpentine."

Morgan laughed out loud.

"It's not that bad. Top me off, would you please?"

The wine had been the valium she'd wished for all night to calm her nerves. She felt herself begin to mellow and relax. It didn't take long before the bottle was empty, and she was thankful for the pepperoni pizza she devoured to help soak up the alcohol.

She sat back in her chair and laid a hand over her stomach.

"Oh my gosh, I'm so stuffed. That was delicious," she said, regretting the last piece she'd gobbled down, leaving her feeling gorged.

She stood and began to clean off the table. Brody got on his feet to stand in front of her.

"Morgan, stop. Frank and I will get this. I'd really like it if you'd stay here with me tonight. If you want to, that is. I can get you to the airport tomorrow."

He squeezed her hand and she looked up into his persuasive green eyes. She felt hypnotized and ready to give in to anything he wanted. She stepped in closer to him and planted her lips on his, using her seduction to answer his question.

If he didn't move this opportunity into the tour bus ASAP, he'd be taking her on top of the dinner table. He had a vision of wine glasses flying to the ground as he cleared the table to have her. He knew she deserved better than that and encouraged her to move inside.

He grabbed Morgan's hand and pulled her up the stairs into the bus. He moved with purpose, not lingering in one place too long. She saw the layout in a blur, twisting and turning her head to take in as much detail as possible. When they reached Brody's private room, he shut the door behind them.

"Well that was quite the tour, Brody. Glad I didn't miss anything," she said with a sarcastic edge.

She took off her jean jacket and set it down on top of the bed, then threw her silver clutch on the nightstand. She looked around the room noting its small size. It was a tight space with a double bed, narrow closet, and a small flat-screen TV mounted on the wall. There were ugly brown curtains over the window beside the bed and absolutely no personal items to be found. A random guitar pick here and there and an empty drinking glass on the nightstand. Brody was sitting on the bed watching her scan the room.

"Come here," he said, grabbing her waist with both hands, gently luring her closer.

"This place could use a woman's touch," she said, as he laid her on the bed and hovered above her.

He brushed a few stray hairs away from her forehead and began trailing kisses along the side of her cheek, working his way down her neck. He paused to sit up for a moment and remove his shirt. His blue jeans rested just below his hips, exposing the sensual hairs that led to his manhood.

Morgan traced her fingertips down the path of hair from his chest, down his torso, reaching the area of allure only to bump into his jeans like an unwanted blockade. She tugged at the button, setting it free, allowing her to pull the zipper down. His growing erection welcomed the release. A surge burst through Morgan's system, forcing her body to come up and meet his. She wrapped her arms around his neck and planted her lips on his, kissing him with aggressive need. Their tongues were deep inside each other when Morgan felt Brody's hand lift her dress and slip his fingers inside her thong. She was wet and moaned at his touch, spreading her legs farther to help facilitate access.

"Jesus, Morgan …" Brody groaned, inserting his finger inside her. Her body accepted the entrance and moved in motion with him. "Take my clothes off, Brody."

He grabbed the bottom of her dress and pulled it over her head. She lay back down on the bed and he grabbed her thong, nearly ripping it in effort to get the thing off. He sat on the edge of the bed to remove his blue jeans and fumbled in the nightstand drawer for a condom.

Morgan's body began to react to the draft in the air. Her nipples tightened and goose bumps spread. Brody stretched over her and brought his mouth down to one nipple, tasting it as she ran her hands through his hair. It didn't take long for his body temperature to take over like a blanket. Morgan wrapped her legs around Brody, manipulating his body in such a way that pleaded for him to take her. Responding to the request, he entered her in one swift movement. She pulled him in closer to her body, holding on tight and breathing heavy.

The small bedroom window fogged over from the humidity projecting out of their bodies. No words had been spoken, just the soft whimpers of release and satisfaction that had been pent up for weeks. Brody rested gently on top of Morgan, while taking a moment to catch his breath, then reached down to draw the sheet over her to prevent a chill. He lay next to her, draping one arm across her stomach.

"I can't wait to do that again," she said.

Brody couldn't think of anything else he'd rather do than make love to Morgan all night long.

CHAPTER THIRTEEN

JUST ALONG FOR THE RIDE

Morgan's eyes slowly crept open as she began to stir. The feel of Brody's warm body against hers became a reminder of where she was. She grabbed his arm, which lay across the top of her thigh, and brought it close to her midsection, wiggling her body to fit inside his like a puzzle piece. Brody slid closer, pushing his lower torso against her. Letting out a sigh of contentment, Morgan reflected on how the movement of the tour bus added a soothing feel, gently rocking them back to sleep.

The lightbulb exploded in her head. Her eyes sprung wide open as she gasped, breaking out of Brody's embrace.

"Oh no no no—this is *not* happening," she said, stretching her arm out to draw open the window blind. "Oh my God—Brody! Wake up! Wake up!" She shook his arm.

"What? What the hell is going on?" he responded, agitated.

"The bus is moving, Brody. *Moving* ... as in we are *not* in LA anymore. I'm supposed to be on a flight back to Denver this afternoon. I don't even know where the hell we are. Oh no.

Ashley's picking me up and if I'm not there ... I have to call her immediately." She fumbled for her cell phone.

"Brody, do you even know where we're headed? This is a mess. All my belongings are back at Brooklyn's apartment. I can't believe ... are you *smiling* right now? Do you seriously think this is funny, Brody Mason?" Her eyes narrowed into his mischievous green ones, which danced up and down in movement with his laughter.

He knew he should be more sensitive to her dilemma but found the situation fucking hilarious. He grabbed her and pulled her close.

"I'm sorry, babe. Everything's going to be fine. We're on our way to San Francisco and I can get you on a flight home then. No big deal."

He leaned in for a kiss, only to get the hand.

"Hold on just a minute, Mr. Sexy Pants. Did you know this would happen?" Morgan asked.

Brody frowned, pondering his response.

"I knew we were heading to San Francisco today, but kidnapping you was not a part of the plan. Relax, Morgan. What's so terrible about having a few extra hours together?" Brody asked, annoyed at her distress.

The corner of her mouth curved into a slight grin. Brody was right. This unforeseen, ridiculous incident was a blessing in disguise. Her tense body began to relax and she bent down to kiss Brody. Her hair fell forward, tickling his face.

His nose twitched as he brought his hands up to comb back the silky strands. He held onto her head so she'd stop for a moment and listen.

"We've got this, Morgan. A few phone calls and everything will be taken care of, okay?"

Morgan smiled in agreement, feeling regretful for overreacting to the situation. *He probably thinks I'm a crazy bitch.*

A muffled commotion outside of Brody's bedroom door caught their attention. Morgan froze, realizing they weren't alone. She could hear Jaxon in the background stirring havoc.

"There's no getting off this bus without getting caught, is there? And … I imagine I'm not the only woman along for the ride, either."

She envisioned the aggressive redhead groping Brody back at the concert arena. The hairs on the back of her neck stuck straight out at the memory.

The smell of coffee drifted through the cracks of the bedroom door, stimulating her senses. She could almost see the steam as it attempted to lure her out of the room. Brody's cell phone vibrated on the nightstand.

"It's Dylan. I need to get this. Go ahead and grab some coffee. I'll be right there."

She looked at Brody, unsure about going out alone. She snuck into the bathroom across the hall to freshen up. Fumbling through the small medicine cabinet, she spotted some toothpaste and used her index finger to brush her teeth. Turning on the faucet, she palmed some water to swish and spit. She lifted her head up to wipe her mouth and the reflection in the mirror scared her.

Good lord—I look like a crackhead.

She found a Q-tip and removed the black eye makeup that had smeared underneath her eyes, leaving a raccoon mask behind. Feeling wrinkled and tacky, she used both hands to brush up and down her dress to smooth out the lines that had settled in from being tossed onto the ground. Her underwear had fortunately been salvaged, saving Morgan from going commando for the rest of the day. She gradually slid open the bathroom pocket door and poked her head out just enough for one eyeball to roam, assessing the area.

"What are you doing, Morgan?"

Jaxon stood across from the bathroom, holding up the wall with his body. His arms were folded across his chest and he displayed a shit-eating grin bigger than the state of Texas. Morgan jumped and her hand flew up to her chest in an attempt to catch her breath.

"Jaxon! You jerk! You scared the crap out of me."

She stepped out of the bathroom and tried to act casual.

"Why are you sneaking around?" Jaxon asked, eyebrows raised.

She shook her head in denial. "I'm not, Jaxon. I was just … well, trying to clean up a little. Why are you lurking in the hallway?" She folded her arms and tilted her head with a cocky snap.

"Leave her alone, Jaxon. You're such an asshole." Brody said as he walked out of the bedroom.

Jaxon laughed, winking at Morgan.

"She knows I'm just giving her shit, Brody. It's about time you got your ass out of bed." He pulled Brody in for a sucker punch to the stomach.

Morgan slid past the two men in an attempt to find the kitchen to score a cup of coffee. Her eyes roamed the tour bus, taking in every detail she'd missed when Brody dragged her through the night before. A sparkle came from the ceiling, where white rope lights were mounted across the borders. She entered the living room to find two black leather bench seats and one recliner.

"Hey—good morning, Morgan." Nate said.

He stood in the small kitchen area, with a coffee mug in one hand and a donut in the other. Breakfast of champions.

Brody and Jaxon stumbled into the room not long after Morgan, bringing a noisy disturbance with them. The two of them shared a brotherly banter that could be considered endearing if only the ruckus that followed didn't exist.

"Donuts? There are donuts, Nate?" Jaxon asked, watching Nate scarf one down. "Where's the box, Nate? Don't hold out on me, man. Cough it up or I'll kick your ass." Jaxon opened cabinet doors to fish around for the box of deep-fried pleasure.

Morgan rolled her eyes and made her way to the coffee maker, pouring herself a generous amount of black liquid energy.

"Morgan, your phone has been going off like crazy. Did you get in touch with Ashley?" Brody asked, handing over her clutch.

"I sent her a text but I haven't checked my phone since. Crap. Two missed calls from her. And several texts from Justin. Hang on while I deal with this."

Morgan turned to head to Brody's bedroom for privacy to call Ashley back.

Ashley answered with a vengeance, causing Morgan to pull her ear away from the phone.

"MOM! What is going on? Are you okay? Where are you?" Her questions came out faster than Morgan could keep up with.

"Everything's fine, honey." Morgan cleared her throat. "It's a pretty funny story, actually. I fell asleep on Brody's tour bus and next thing I know I'm headed for San Francisco."

Dead silence.

"Ashley ... are you with me?"

"So, what you're telling me is that you slept on a bus, with the band, and you are NOT on your way home," Ashley said, less than amused.

"I didn't sleep with *the band*. Just ... Brody."

Geez—this isn't coming out right.

"Anyway, Brody set up a flight for me out of the San Francisco airport. I'll text you my flight info. If you can't pick me up, I'll take a shuttle." Her tone turned defensive. "I feel like I'm in trouble or something here. The fact is, I'm not required to explain myself to you."

Not wanting to quarrel with her daughter, she adjusted her attitude.

Ashley broke the awkward silence between them. "I'll be at the airport when you get in. Have a safe flight, Mom."

Morgan turned off her phone and sat down on Brody's bed, dreading what was coming next. Another round of goodbyes surrounded by question marks. Her mind swirled, contemplating what to do about their situation. Should she say "Hey, thanks for the sex" and cut all ties with Brody, or allow him to leave her hanging with false hope?

I should never have come. Why did I do this to myself? She felt sick to her stomach.

There was a light knock on the door, then Brody poked his head in.

"Hey. Everything okay in here? You've been gone a while."

"Oh yeah … fine. Um, by the way, are there any other stowaways on this bus besides me? Just trying to prevent myself from being blindsided. Not that it's any of my business who else spends the night, but I'm not excited about running into groping Barbie." Jealousy rearing its ugly head.

Brody shut the door behind him and maneuvered Morgan to lie down on the bed as he hovered above her.

"You have been such a pill. I think I must bring the worst out in you," Brody teased, smiling down at her.

"Geez—I know. You're right. I'm so sorry. What is wrong with me? I'm usually so nice and—"

Brody put his fingers across her lips.

"Shhh … you're human, Morgan. I find this side of you sexy as hell. I'm just giving you shit."

Brody planted his lips on hers and lunged his tongue inside. All Morgan could think about was how good he tasted and how much she wanted him. He didn't bring out the worst in her. He brought her to *life*, making her feel sexy and wanted. Passion had been a lost existence, feeling more and more unretrievable. But now… now, Brody had reawakened her sexuality.

Brody pushed himself up to release some of his weight off of Morgan. His green eyes narrowed in on her like a spotlight.

"Groping Barbie? Now that's one I've never heard before."

"Stop it, Brody. Don't make fun. I could have called her much worse."

Brody grabbed Morgan's arms, pulling her to a sitting position. "Well, the coast is clear. Let's go eat. I'm starving! We could both use some fuel."

* * *

The rest of the morning flew by and before Morgan knew it, the tour bus was pulling into San Francisco. She'd been curled up on the leather couch looking out the window for miles but had no recollection of what she'd seen. She'd gone over and over in her head how to play things out with Brody when it was time to leave.

Brody joined her on the couch, settling himself up against her back as she continued her trance through the looking glass. He kissed the side of her head and spoke softly into her ear.

"We'll be there soon. There will be a car waiting to take you to the airport when we get to the concert arena."

Brody stroked the side of her arm, moving up and down as if trying to warm her up. It was a gesture of compassion—he knew all too well the fight she was battling in her head.

"I think it would be best if I don't go to the airport with you, Morgan. I feel like an asshole not escorting you there, but—"

Morgan turned around to face Brody, forcing a smile to surface that wasn't the least bit convincing.

"I agree, Brody. Why make this any harder than it already is."

Jaxon, Nate, and Johnny bustled over a card game in the background.

"You cheat, Jaxon! I don't know why I always play with you." Johnny bitched at his bandmate.

"You're just being a sore loser because I won all of your snack-size Hershey's miniatures. Now, fork them over fair and square," Jaxon demanded, rubbing it in.

Nate threw his cards down on the table, blowing out a defeated breath.

"I'm done here. You cleaned me out, Jaxon. I hope your teeth rot."

"Hahahaha—suckers!" Jaxon teased as he swiped his winnings off of the table.

"I stopped gambling with Jaxon a long time ago, you guys. He's a classic hustler. You should know better by now. Suck it up." Brody said, poking fun at his friends.

"I'm not stupid, you know. Chicks love chocolate. I keep it stashed in my room. By the way, Brody, I think you just gave me a backhanded compliment. Being a hustler takes brains and imagination. Two more things chicks like. Man, I am one lucky son of a bitch." Jaxon stood up from the table to stretch.

"Everything in this bus is like tiny-house living for me. Gets hard on the body after a while. Fuck!" His back cracked from one vertebra to another.

Feeling grateful for the distraction, Morgan found herself laughing at Jaxon and his antics. He was a big kid at heart, trapped inside a man's body.

She felt the bus slow down and a make a right turn into a large parking lot. She looked out the window and reality hit. *This is where I get off.* A black town car was parked in the distance and the bus headed straight for it.

"Well, I'd gather up my things, but … I don't have any. It's a good thing I thought to put my ID in my clutch before Brooklyn and I left for the concert. This will be the lightest I've ever traveled."

The tour bus came to a screeching halt. Frank opened the doors and a cool breeze drifted through.

"Come on. I'll walk you out." Brody said, touching Morgan's back as they moved forward. She stopped and turned back around.

"See you around guys. Have a great tour. Try to stay out of trouble, Jaxon." She smiled and threw a wink his way.

"See ya, Morgan. You can get stuck on our bus any time," Nate said.

As soon as Brody and Morgan reached the car, the rest of the band ran over to the window to watch like Peeping Toms.

"Back up! Back up! Geez! They're going to see one of us." Jaxon wailed.

"Shhhh. What do you think Brody's going to do? He can't just let her get away again. Right? I mean, he's not that stupid, is he?" Johnny asked.

"You guys are as bad as a bunch of old biddies gossiping in front of the grocery store. Pathetic," Frank chastised, shaking his head in disbelief. "Shall I grab the binoculars for you? That way you can read lips and shit like that."

"Shut up, Frank! We're concentrating here," Jaxon growled, waving his arm at him to chill.

Brody shoved one hand in his pocket and the other scratched the back of his head.

"Here we are again, huh?" he said, his expression apologetic.

Pulling his hand out of his pocket, he reached for Morgan and reeled her in for an embrace. Fighting back tears that were pulsing to escape, she held him tight. He released her and rested his forehead against hers.

"Morgan ... I don't want to leave things the way I did last time. It was so cold and—"

She stopped him before he could finish. She opened her clutch and took out her cell phone.

"Give me your phone number, Brody. Right now."

He looked at her puzzled as his spouted off numbers.

"I'm calling your phone. You have my number and I have yours. There are no excuses. If you want to talk, call me. There's no pressure. I'm not going to stalk you."

She stood on her tiptoes to kiss him goodbye.

"The ball's in your court, Brody. I won't chase you around the country."

She bent down to climb into the back seat of the car. Brody held onto the door, his arm frozen to shut it. Squatting, he stared at her as if he wasn't finished with their conversation.

"Morgan—"

"Thank you for everything, Brody. I ... I have to go," she said.

She reached her arm past him to grab the handle of the car door. Brody reluctantly stepped aside. He knew that he hadn't said enough, but she'd practically shut the door on him.

Morgan made eye contact with the driver through the rearview mirror.

"Let's go. Quickly, please," she said, her expression desperate.

She closed her eyes and forced herself not to turn around and look at Brody through the back window.

* * *

"Johnny, can you back the fuck off? I can feel your nasty breath in my ear and it's freaking me out," Jaxon bitched.

The boys had remained huddled by the window, spying intently.

"Guys—Brody's heading this way. Shit—scatter!" Nate ordered.

Jaxon moved quickly, hitting his head on the cabinet above him.

"Fuck!"

"Shut up, Jaxon. Make yourself look productive. Hurry. Go grab your drumsticks and bang on shit or something," Johnny begged.

Brody entered the tour bus, acting casual as he shut the door behind him. The first thing he noticed how quiet it was. Nate was on the couch with a book in hand, while Johnny and Jaxon were fumbling through the kitchen cabinets as if they were looking for something.

"You guys are really bad at being inconspicuous. Nate ... a book? Really? Suddenly interested in picking up reading?"

"So ... Morgan is gone. I'm not about to go off the deep end. I know what's going on here and you don't have to worry. Now let's get ready to show San Francisco we can still kick ass."

"Hell, yeah!" Jaxon said, punching his arms into the air. He grabbed Brody around the neck in a chokehold.

"I love you, man."

CHAPTER FOURTEEN

SURVIVING THE STORM

"Ashley, would you please stop pacing around? You're making me crazy." Justin rubbed his hands over his face.

"I can't help it. Mom's fragile right now and God knows what happened on that bus. Justin? Are you listening to me? Maybe if you took your eyes off that phone—"

"Just hold on a sec," Justin said, holding his hand up to push pause. "Mom's plane just landed. Try to calm down before she comes walking through that gate."

The Denver airport was a major flight hub. People of all kinds speed walking to make connections, retrieve luggage, or be greeted by family. Heads weaving in and out. A faint sound of a child's cry rolled through the air. Traveling took its toll at times. Ashley tapped her foot nervously, waiting to spot her mom.

"Oh—I see her! Mom!" Ashley waved, trying to catch Morgan's attention. Justin got up from his seat to stand next to his sister.

"Wow, she looks ... hmmm ... a little haggard. Must have been quite a ride," he teased, rocking back and forth on his heels.

Ashley nudged him in the side, making him cough out loud.

Morgan stopped to stand in front of Justin and Ashley, bearing only her small silver clutch.

"Hey, thank you so much for picking me up. It's been a long day and I'm whipped." Morgan extended an arm to hug Ashley.

"Whoa, Mom. You are in serious need of a shower." Ashley said.

"Gee ... you think? I've been in the same clothes for the last twenty-four hours." Morgan's tone had gone from pleasant to grumpy.

"Never mind that. Let's go get your things at baggage claim," Justin suggested.

"This is all I have. The rest of my things are at Brooklyn's in Venice Beach and I don't want to talk about it. Let's just go home, okay?"

Justin wrapped his arm around Morgan's shoulder, as Ashley led the way to the parking garage. The ride home was quiet, with only the hum of the heater making a sound. Morgan sat in the back seat of the car, arms folded across her stomach, head resting against the cold window. Ashley looked back at her mom from the front seat. She wanted to speak but was frozen to do so. Everything in Morgan's body language discouraged conversation.

Justin's Lexus eased into the driveway. Morgan blew out a long breath and opened her door to step out. Once inside the house, she paused to face her children.

"I'm beat you guys. I just want to shower and go straight to bed. We can all talk in the morning. Thank you for picking me up. I love you. Goodnight."

Justin and Ashley responded at the same time.

"Goodnight, Mom."

Morgan turned and headed for her bedroom, gently shutting the door behind her. The faint click of the door alerted Ashley that her mom was out of hearing range.

"God, I hate seeing Mom this way. This affair or whatever it is she has going on with Brody is toxic. What should we do?" She turned to her brother for guidance.

"We aren't going to do anything until Mom asks us to, Ashley. She's trying to stand on her own. This thing with Brody was unforeseen ... she even said so. I think it started out as a good time and then ... got complicated." Justin's words were suddenly interrupted by the ringing of Ashley's cell phone.

"It's Brooklyn. I'm going to take this in my room and talk to her for a bit. Hey, Brooklyn ..." Ashley's voice trailed off into the distance as she walked downstairs to her room.

Justin walked over to Morgan's bedroom door and rested his ear against it. He didn't know what he was listening for but felt satisfied at the sound of running water from the shower.

She'll feel better in the morning.

His hand touched the door in an endearing way before he quietly snuck off to his own room for the night.

* * *

Morgan wiped the steam off the bathroom mirror and towel-dried her hair. Picking up a wide-tooth comb, she worked out the tangles.

"I'm a hot mess," she said, looking at herself in the mirror.

A good night's sleep beckoned as she rummaged through the dresser drawer to find comfy clothes to slip into. The sound of her cell phone vibrating on the nightstand diverted her attention.

I need to turn that damn thing off for the night.

She walked over to the nightstand and picked up her phone to see who was intruding on her mission to go to bed. Her eyes popped open in surprise, jolting her out of her sleepiness.

Brody.

She opened the text message and read intently: *Hey, Morgan. Just checking to make sure you made it home safe.*

She could hear Brody's voice inside her head as she read the text. Morgan began to type her response, then she paused for a moment. Feeling inspired, she stopped texting and hit the call button.

"Hey, Brody. I made it fine. Tell me all about San Francisco."

* * *

The next morning, Ashley, still in her pajamas, banged around in the kitchen in an effort to make breakfast. Clanking skillets and the gurgling of the coffee pot had awakened Justin like a rooster calling.

Who needs an alarm clock around here?

Stumbling out of bed, he followed the sounds of the disturbance.

"Good morning. I need coffee. What are you making anyway?" he asked, scoping out the mad scene.

"Justin … have you seen my favorite whisk? I can't work without it. It should be right here in this drawer." Ashley carried on, pulling open every drawer in the kitchen.

He rolled his eyes and poured himself a mug of coffee.

"It's too early for this, sis. Can't do it."

At that moment, Morgan came barreling out of her room, a backpack draped around her shoulder. She wore blue jeans and hiking boots and had layered her upper body to prepare for cold temperatures.

"Hey … good morning. I need a heavy coat for the day. Is there one in the hallway closet?" she asked.

Ashley froze, looking confused. Waving a black spatula around in the air, she began the interrogation.

"What is going on, Mom? Where are you going?" She looked over at Justin with furrowed eyebrows.

"Here's one. Perfect! I'm heading out to Estes Park to take some photographs. It's time to get back to work."

"By yourself? You know, Estes Park is like an hour and a half away," Ashley said. "Why don't you go to Lost Lake instead, Mom. Boulder County is closer."

"Because—I did my research. I want cliffs and ruggedness. I'll do Lost Lake another day. Thanks for the tip, honey." Morgan walked over to Ashley to plant a big kiss on her cheek.

"I love how you worry about me. But … don't. Be happy for me. I'm inspired and ready to spread my wings."

"That's great, Mom," Justin said. "Just give us a time frame in case we need to come looking for you. You would ask the same of us."

Zipping up the gray down coat, Morgan picked up her backpack and headed for the front door.

"I'll be home by dark. See ya!" She waved and flew out the front door like an excited child.

Ashley didn't move, staring at the front door long after Morgan left. Justin reached around her statuesque body and grabbed a piece of bacon that had been getting cold. Oil began popping from the sizzling skillet on the burner, causing him to step back.

"The rest of the bacon is going to burn, Ashley. Better get on that," he teased as he crunched away on the salty pork.

Smiling as he walked past her, Justin felt amused by her state of unease. He could feel her eyes narrowing in on him like daggers.

"Love you," he said, turning his head to wink at her before heading into his bedroom.

* * *

Morgan parked her SUV and decided to send Ashley a text. *Made it to Estes Park. Going to take the Alberta Falls Trail. Love you.*

Gathering up her backpack, Morgan began her trek. The sun hit her forehead like a laser, causing her to squint. Holding a hand up to provide shade to her face, Morgan retrieved her sunglasses from her pocket.

Not a cloud in sight.

The air felt brisk on her cheeks and the humidity projected from her mouth every time she exhaled. After a half mile or so into the hike, her layers of clothing got to be too much.

"This looks like a good place to stop," she said.

Setting her backpack down against a large Douglas fir tree, Morgan removed her down coat. Her white long-sleeved thermal t-shirt felt sufficient, as she pushed the sleeves up to her elbows. Pulling out her water bottle from the pack, she chugged down several gulps, thankful for the hydration. She stood with her hands on her hips for a moment, taking advantage of this precious opportunity. The forest was dense in front of her, but as she stepped out toward the cliff's edge, she could see for miles. She spotted the waterfalls from a distance.

"*That* is where I need to be," she said. "Just a little ways more."

Grabbing her things, she continued the hike until she found the waterfalls.

Not wanting to waste any time, she assembled her camera and let the creativity take over. There were trees and boulders all around the falls. The lighting couldn't have been any better. The sun projected enough light, while playing hide and seek amongst the trees. The crashing sound of the water as it hit the surface of the river flooded the atmosphere. She could feel light bursts of water on her forearms as she got closer.

Balancing herself on a large boulder, she focused her camera and clicked away, hoping to capture the spray as the water bounced off the rocks. She concentrated intently, not wanting to miss a single opportunity, when all of a sudden she felt something hit the back of her head.

"Don't. Move."

Morgan paused as her heart began to race furiously. A man had a gun to her head. Her eyes roamed the area. Not a soul in sight. Not good.

"Turn around slowly. No fast moves or else," the gunman ordered in a raspy voice.

Lowering her camera, Morgan stuck her arms out to the side and pivoted around to face the gunman. She sucked in a quick breath at his scary presence. He stood tall, with dirty brown hair and a scruffy five-day shadow. Crow's feet in the corner of his eyes gave him a weathered appearance, as well as the speckles of gray hair around his temples.

Morgan began to memorize every last detail of the man threatening her. Eyes so dark they were nearly black. He wore blue jeans and a red-and-black flannel t-shirt underneath a blue jean jacket. Her eyes locked on the black semiautomatic pistol pointed right at her chest.

"You're coming with me. I saw your pack. We're going to get it and move on. Now *go!*" The stranger nudged her in the back to lead the way.

Morgan found the Douglas fir bracing her pack and bent down in an attempt to put her camera away. The gunman grabbed her arm tight.

"Don't even think about pulling something on me, girl."

Trying to remain calm, she held her hands up in the air. "I'm just putting the camera away. Then I need to put my coat on. That's it. Please ... let go of me."

The gunman hesitantly let go of her arm and shoved the semiautomatic into her back as she packed the camera. Zipping up the backpack, she picked up her coat.

"I can't put my coat on with that pistol stuck to my back. Do you mind?" Morgan said in a sarcastic tone.

Her inner voice exploded with a warning.

Careful, Morgan. You are going to get yourself killed.

He stepped back to give Morgan a little room. That's when she noticed his brown cowboy boots.

Interesting choice of shoes for a hike. This man is not supposed to be out here.

"Move it, lady. We don't have all day. And stay off the fucking trail. This way ..." The man waved his gun in the opposite direction.

They walked and walked for what felt like miles. The only sound to be heard was the crunching of pine needles and leaves on the ground from their shoes.

Morgan slowed down her pace, finally coming to a stop.

"What are you doing, lady? We need to keep moving."

Holding her hands up in the air, she challenged the dark-eyed gunman.

"What's the plan here? I don't know where we're going. We're just walking ... to what? The sun will be going down eventually and then …? We'll freeze out here. Have you thought of that?" she said with a cocky head tilt.

"Shut up, bitch!" he said, swinging at her with his semiautomatic and striking her left cheekbone.

Morgan fell to the ground, a burning sensation pulsing through her face.

"Get up and keep moving! We stop when I say. Got that?"

Morgan got to her feet and proceeded on. Her mind went around and around, trying to find a way out of this mess. Things weren't looking good. The temperature was beginning to drop and would continue to do so.

She thought of her kids and … and realized her cell phone was zipped in her coat pocket. There was a possibility she could be found by GPS.

When I don't show up at home after dark, Ashley will be on the horn. Without a doubt.

Morgan just had to keep her mouth shut and stay alive.

* * *

BREAKING NEWS … BREAKING NEWS! flashed across every flat-screen TV at the Denver brewery. Ashley strutted from table to table, not missing a beat. A tray of several glasses of craft beer balanced in one hand and a plate of appetizers hung off her other arm as she headed for a rowdy group of guys at a high-top.

"Here you go, boys. Enjoy. Can I get you anything else?" she asked, distributing extra napkins all around and flashing a flirty grin. Both were essential for scoring good tips.

She could feel her cell phone blowing up in her back pocket.

"Just wave me down if you need anything else." She turned on her heels to find an appropriate place to check her phone messages. Two missed calls from Justin and several texts.

What the hell is going on?

The last text read, *CHECK THE NEWS! HURRY.*

Ashley ran for the closest flat-screen. She grabbed the remote and cranked up the volume. The trailer at the bottom of the screen read: *Armed robber believed to have fled into Estes Park. Park has been shut down as police begin their search.*

"Oh my God. Mom!"

Tearing off her apron, she fled the restaurant, calling Justin in the process.

"Justin, we have to notify the police."

"I already have. We need to head to Estes Park where they've set up a search camp nearby. Stay there and I'll pick you up. I'm on my way. Call Brooklyn. We need to get her out here."

Ashley hung up her cell and immediately dialed her sister.

"Come on, Brooklyn. Answer … answer please."

* * *

"We need to stop for a water break. I can't go any further," Morgan begged.

"Give me your pack." the gunman responded.

Morgan sat down on the cold ground as he fumbled through the backpack, finally retrieving the water bottle. Pulling it out, he tossed the pack down on the ground by her feet. He opened the cap and guzzled down every last drop. Wiping the dregs from his chin, he smiled down at her.

"Well, now. Looks like there's none left for you, little lady. Hahahaha ..." The gunman laughed harder and harder as his chest bounced up and down.

Morgan could barely see out of her left eye from the swelling. She could see just enough of the horrible man waving his gun around and making fun of her. Signs of dehydration alerted her. She felt weak and her head hurt like hell.

The gunman stuck his head right into her face, exposing his rotten teeth and rancid breath.

"Poor baby—no pouting now. Get up. Get *up*, I said."

Morgan used her hands to push herself up off the ground. She felt helpless and defeated. The son of a bitch had no conscience, no morals. Reality was, he would most likely kill her.

* * *

"We have to get my Mom out of there, Captain." Ashley begged, holding on to Justin's hand.

They stood under a tent near Estes Park, trying to find the patience to sit back and wait for information. A team of police, along with Search and Rescue, bustled around, conversing on their walkie-talkies.

"Come over here and take a look at this," the Captain said, directing them to a map spread out on a table.

"GPS has tracked your mom's phone right about here." He circled the area of the map with his pencil.

"This is a long way off from where she allegedly started this morning. She isn't on any trails any more. If she'd intended to only be gone for the day, it's not likely she would have hiked out this far. That being said, the top two possibilities are number one—she's lost or injured. Or number two—worst-case scenario—our armed robber, Jameson Ray, has taken her hostage to protect himself. We have a team closing in on her location. They're trained for this very thing. It's a waiting game at this point. Please ... try to hang in there."

Justin turned to face Ashley and held on to both of her hands.

"Hey. I know you're scared. We have to stay positive for Mom. Do you know if Brooklyn was able to get a flight out here?" he said.

"I ... I don't know. She was working on it the last time we talked."

"Why don't you check in with her. I'll hang close here for anything new to come up, okay?" He planted a kiss on the top of her head.

* * *

"Jaxon ... how's the sound from over there?" Brody asked as he tuned his guitar. "It's not sounding right to my ear, man."

Jaxon lay stretched across the sofa, his long skinny legs dangling over the end, tossing a football up into the air and catching it—over and over.

"Yeah man ... play a riff or two just to make sure," Jaxon said, holding onto the ball to give Brody his undivided attention.

Swinging his legs around, he got up from the couch and grabbed his sticks. Crouching in front of Brody, Jaxon looked around to see who was in earshot.

"What is it, Jaxon? Something up?" Brody asked as he strummed his guitar.

"Oh ... you know, bro ... just wondering if you've talked to Morgan?"

Brody stopped strumming and looked his friend in the eye.

"I called her today."

Jaxon shook his head.

"So ... that's it? You called her, and ...? You're killing me here, dude."

Right at that moment, the door to the tour bus swung open. Dylan entered, stomping toward the flat-screen TV. He surfed channels until he found CNN.

"Jesus, Dylan. What the fuck?" Jaxon asked.

"Something's going on with Morgan, that's what ... and it's not good. Dad, come here and take a look."

Brody set his guitar down and moved in closer to the TV screen. Jaxon followed, hovering behind him. The room was so quiet you could hear a pin drop as they read the headlines and listened to the news reporter.

"Holy shit, Brody. You said you talked to her today," Jaxon said, confusion in his tone.

"No ... I said I called her. She didn't answer. Now I know why."

"Dad, Brooklyn says Morgan is either lost in there or taken hostage by that madman." Dylan pointed his index finger to the picture on the screen.

"It's almost dark. If they don't find her soon … shit, Brody." Jaxon laid his hand on Brody's shoulder.

Brody stood frozen staring at the TV screen. The rage began to build inside. He looked down at the ground and both hands turned into fists. His expression became taut as his eyes squinted and his lips curled in. A mad bulldog would describe it. Not quite foaming at the mouth.

"Dad, I know that look. Try to keep it together."

"If that son of a bitch lays one hand on her, I'm going to destroy him. Dylan, we're going to Denver. I want to be on a plane—like right this damn minute."

* * *

Dusk had displayed itself over the top of Estes Park, like a black ghost floating in. Morgan's ears and cheeks were red from the cold air. The more steps she took, the more her legs felt like concrete blocks. They had begun to resist her demands.

The gunman tugged the back of her coat, catching a handful of her hair along with it. Her neck jerked back and her feet stumbled.

Pointing to a decline in the terrain, the gunman gave orders.

"We're heading right down there for the night."

He pushed Morgan forward and her feet lost traction from the dry pine needles on the ground. She felt herself going down and stuck her hands out behind her to brace her fall. She skidded a bit, the palms of her hands dragging and scraping the ground.

The gunman came up behind her and dragged her off the ground, pulling her arm fiercely.

"Clumsy woman. You're worthless." He spit on the ground in disgust.

A voice on a bullhorn came from the woods.

"Jameson Ray—we have targets all over you. Put the gun down and step aside right now."

The gunman's expression lit up in surprise and he lunged for Morgan. He pulled her close against him, pointing the semiautomatic into the side of her head.

"I will kill her. Back off or I WILL kill her."

Morgan spotted not one, but half a dozen men dressed in black combat gear, circling their perimeter, pointing rifles right at the gunman. Now identified as Jameson Ray.

"Give up, Jameson. Drop your weapon and let the woman go. Drop it now. This is your last warning. I repeat, your last warning," the voice projected from the bullhorn.

Jameson hugged Morgan tighter to his body and leaned his head in close to her ear. He cleared his throat and whispered in a malicious gruff tone.

"Looks like this is the end for you. Say your prayers, lady."

Morgan closed her eyes and took a deep breath. Tears were streaming down her cheeks when—

BOOM!

CHAPTER FIFTEEN

DESPERATE MEASURES

"I have eyes on the target. Waiting for confirmation to fire my weapon, sir," the sniper spoke.

"Roger that. We want Jameson and the hostage out alive if possible. Just hold on ..." the Captain responded.

The sniper, perched lying low to the ground, had a red laser light locked right in between Jameson Ray's eyes.

"Ray is going to shoot, sir. Requesting permission to fire immediately." The sniper's voice rose, desperation in his tone.

Jameson's trigger finger began to curl slowly as he pushed the semiautomatic harder into the side of Morgan's head.

"Firing my weapon!" the sniper called out.

BOOM! The sound of an explosion burst through the trees and echoed across the canyon walls. Birds scattered, strewing leaves about and leaving behind an eerie silence.

The S.W.A.T. team moved quickly, closing in on Morgan to extract her from the deadly scene before her. She hadn't yet opened her eyes, but she could feel the perpetrator's body limp against her leg.

"Ms. Gray, come with me. We're going take good care of you and get you out of here. Everything's going to be fine." The man's voice spoke gently as he reached for her arm.

The rest of the S.W.A.T. team had guns pointed on the gunman, while one bent down to check for a pulse.

"Jameson Ray confirmed dead, sir. I repeat, the target is deceased," he said into his shoulder radio.

"Good work, team. What's the status of our hostage?" the Captain asked.

"Lacerations to the face and dehydration, sir. Requesting Search and Rescue to bring in helicopter to remove hostage and transport to nearest hospital."

"Roger that. Hang tight ... sending copter in."

* * *

Justin held Ashley as they waited in fear under the Search and Rescue tent. The air had become piercingly colder as the sun continued to go down. A shiver ran through Ashley when she noticed the sound of footsteps approaching. Her head turned to follow the sound, finding the Captain approaching them. Ashley's eyes opened wide as Justin squeezed her tight, listening intently.

"We sent a S.W.A.T. team in to search for the gunman, Jameson Ray. He robbed a convenience store earlier this morning. Ditched his car and fled into Estes Park. Your mom was in the wrong place at the wrong time. He took her hostage as insurance, so to speak. A way out. Our sniper fired on Jameson when he believed your mom was going to get shot. S.W.A.T. confirmed Ray's death not long ago, requesting a helicopter rescue for your mom. She will be flown directly to the Denver hospital."

"Hospital? What happened to her? Is she going to be all right?" Ashley asked, panic building.

"I believe so, but I don't have all the information. She's dehydrated and has some injuries. You should be prepared—she may be in shock. They will take good care of her. Best you be on your way to the hospital. She'll need you." The Captain rested his hand on Justin's shoulder.

"Thank you, Captain." Justin reached out to shake his hand.

"Send a text out to Brooklyn, Ash, so she knows where to head when her plane lands. Ashley?" Justin asked, a bit concerned that his sister was in a state of shock as well.

He reached for her shoulders and looked square into her eyes.

"Hey ... Mom is going to be fine. She's safe."

"Yeah ... okay. I ... um ... I'm fine. I'll text Brooklyn as soon as we get into the car. Let's go," Ashley responded, her stride intense as she headed for Justin's Lexus.

* * *

Brody didn't waste any time chartering a private jet to Denver. One of the perks of being famous and rich.

"I told Frank to take the tour bus on to Oregon. The guys will prepare for the next show until they hear otherwise. Once we land, I'll try to pin down Brooklyn for more details," Dylan said.

Brody sat in his seat, one leg resting on top of the other, staring out the window at the clouds resting in the air like pillows.

"I should've been more open with her. I just let her leave in that damn town car, brooding and feisty. Shit!"

Dylan bent down to access the bar freezer, extracting two large squares of ice. He grabbed two glasses from the shelf, dropped the cubes in, and poured whiskey in each.

"Here you go, Dad. This will take the edge off for a bit."

He took a seat across from Brody and leaned back to decompress. His long legs stretched out, he blew out a breath and ran his hand through his hair. He took one sip of his whiskey and stared into the glass, swirling the ice around before throwing back the rest.

A voice from the flight deck came over the cabin speaker.

"We are about to make our descent into Denver International. Please remain in your seat with your seat belts fastened. We thank you for flying with us today."

Brody glanced over at Dylan, looking to him for support.

"This is it."

* * *

"Mom … Mom, can you hear me? Justin and I are right here with you." Ashley combed her fingers through Morgan's hair.

A woman in blue scrubs, sporting a dark-brown French twist secured at the back of her head, entered the room.

"Hi there. I'm your Mom's nurse. My name is Jen," she said, flitting around like the Energizer bunny.

Ashley stepped back, allowing Jen to check vitals and fluids.

"Why won't she wake up? She *will* wake up won't she?" Ashley asked.

"Oh, she's going to be just fine honey. Your mom has been through a lot. Doc will be in shortly to go over everything with you."

"Ashley, Brooklyn is here," Justin said, stepping out of the room to greet his youngest sis.

Brooklyn entered the room and the three of them stood around Morgan's hospital bed in a quiet vigil.

"Look at her face. What did that son of a bitch do to her?" Brooklyn asked, walking over to get a closer look.

"She's lucky to be alive," came a voice from behind them.

"Hello. I'm Dr. Buchanan. Forgive my intrusion. I thought I would get you up to date. Your Mom is going to be fine. Tests show that there is no concussion from the obvious head trauma, but she came in pretty dehydrated. I would like to keep her overnight. Make sure she is stable when she wakes up."

"Um … thank you, Doctor. I'm the oldest daughter, Ashley. Nice to meet you." She flashed a gentle grin, eyelashes batting up and down at an unusually fast speed. *My my … young and hot*, she thought.

"Ashley, you can stop shaking his hand now." Brooklyn rolled her eyes.

"Of course … haha … sorry. I'm just *so* relieved and thankful. Thank you so much, Dr. Buchanan." Ashley tried to cover the fact that she was flirting. Brooklyn continued to watch her sister's antics, shaking her head and laughing inside.

* * *

"I hate the smell of hospitals. Makes me want to throw up," Dylan said, following close behind Brody's determined heels.

"*Excuse* me, gentlemen. Can I help you?" a nurse asked, chasing them down the hall.

"You can't just come barging in here. What do you need?"

Brody stopped short and pivoted his body toward the bitchy nurse.

Oh no, Dylan thought, reaching out to grab his dad's arm.

"Dad, don't. You'll get us kicked out of here."

Brody caught himself before speaking and cleared his throat.

"Morgan Gray. We're here to see Morgan Gray." He looked square into the nurse's eyes, challenging her to even think about stopping him from finding Morgan.

"Around the corner to the left. Room two-twenty, I believe. You know, there are already quite a few people in there. Maybe you should just … never mind. Please, continue."

"Thank you. Come on, Dad." Dylan said, tugging on Brody's arm to move on.

"What the hell was that all about? Chasing us down like we … are …" Brody's rant stood uncompleted when he reached Morgan's room.

Brooklyn spotted Dylan and charged out of the hospital room to reach him. A few strides and she was in his arms. Brody walked past them and paused at the doorway, waiting for permission from Ashley and Justin to step in.

"Brody! Hey, come on in. Mom's starting to stir a bit. She's been out for a while," Justin said.

Brody shook Justin's hand and walked over to Morgan's bedside. He reached out to pick up her hand, wedging it between his own.

"Ashley, let's go grab a bite in the cafeteria," Justin suggested.

"Go on. I'm not hungry," she said, clueless.

"Yes … you … are." Justin repeated, clearing his throat and throwing suggestive eye movements Ashley's way.

"Oh … yes. I am famished, actually. We'll be right back, Brody." Tilting her head a notch, she squinted at Justin and whispered to him on the way out the door.

"I'm not stupid. I get it."

* * *

Brody set Morgan's hand down and reached out to stroke his fingers across the laceration on her left cheek. The swelling had taken over around her eye, causing it to look nearly sewn shut.

"Hey sweetheart," he said, the emotions building up inside. "I'm so sorry this happened to you. You … you were so brave and …" Brody was paralyzed to continue, getting more choked up by the second.

He cleared his throat. "I love you."

Leaning over Morgan, he kissed her forehead.

"So this is what it takes to get Brody Mason to come clean, huh?" Morgan said, her voice dry and raspy.

Brody's upper body shot back as he looked down at her.

"Jesus, Morgan. If I wasn't so damned happy you're awake I'd be pissed right now. You kind of scared the shit out of me. Thought I was … well … kind of talking to myself right now."

"Hmm, I see. So you don't want me to know you love me," she teased.

"That's not what … forget it. How are you? You've given all of us a scare." He looked out the doorway to catch Dylan's attention, waving him inside.

Dylan grabbed Brooklyn's hand, and led her inside Morgan's room.

"Mom! You're awake. Oh my God. Just … let me text Justin and Ashley real quick. How are you? How do you feel? Dylan, we should get the nurse. Please."

"Sure … great … another nurse. Noooo problem," he said, hesitating to head to the nurses' station.

Brody nodded at him to get moving.

"Mom, do you remember anything? Do you know why you're here?" Brooklyn asked.

"Yes … um … I was in Estes Park and …. that man took me. They killed him. He *is* dead, right?"

Brooklyn nodded.

"Yes, Mom. He's dead. He'll never hurt you again."

Justin and Ashley stumbled in, nearly getting stuck together in the doorway. Justin pushed Ashley through first, then followed.

"Mom!"

Brody and Brooklyn stepped out of the way to clear a path.

"Where is that nurse?" Brooklyn asked.

Ashley tuned into her sister's distress and raised her hand like a child in a classroom.

"Ooh … I would be more than happy to go find Doctor Buchanan. Yep, we definitely need him right now. I'm on it. Be right back, Mom. So glad you're awake."

Ashley brushed past Brooklyn and fled the room like a spinning tornado.

"Justin, I want to go home," Morgan said. "What do we have to do to make that happen?"

"Don't be in a rush, Mom. You need fluids and rest. Doc says when you go home, okay? As soon as we get the thumbs-up, I'll take you home. I promise."

Brody paced the room, glancing at Brooklyn and Justin before he spoke. He stopped to stand at the foot of Morgan's bed, hands on his hips, looking very serious.

"Morgan, I want you to go on tour with me."

Brooklyn and Justin looked at each other, shocked.

"What? No—absolutely *not*," Morgan responded.

Brody bent down and rested his hands on the rail of the bed, glaring into her eyes. *Like hell she won't*, he thought, the steam brewing.

Ashley burst into the room out of breath.

"I … I couldn't find him. By the way, Brooklyn, some nurse has Dylan prisoner back there." She gestured her thumb toward the hall.

"What's going on? What did I miss?" Ashley asked, taking note of the distress bouncing around the room.

Morgan redirected her eyes away from Ashley to stare Brody down. She knew that stance, that body language.

"Brody. There's no way I'm going on tour with you. Mm... mmm. Nope. *Not* happening ..."

CHAPTER SIXTEEN

WHEN A WOMAN SAYS NO, IT MEANS YES

Three Months Later

"All right guys. This will make a great pic for the Facebook page. Perfect—really. That's a wrap!" Morgan said, adjusting her camera.

"Thank God. It's fucking freezing out here, Morgan." Jaxon whined. "Chicago in the winter is brutal."

She walked over to stand with the members of Keyed Up and take in the view of Lake Michigan.

"Jaxon, take a look out there. It's fabulous. That body of water they refer to as a 'lake.' It blows my mind," she said, encouraging him to appreciate the moment.

Brody walked up behind her and wrapped his arms around her stomach.

"You've done an amazing job, babe. Because of you, we'll have the best-documented concert tour ever. The feedback has been unreal. Thank you." He leaned in to kiss the side of her cheek.

He stopped to look at the scar left behind from her terrible ordeal. All he could think about was how he wanted to protect Morgan. Keep her in his pocket.

"I have to admit, Brody. It's been the best experience. I should be thanking you." She squeezed his arm.

Morgan had flooded the social network in every arena promoting the *Behind Closed Doors* concert tour with her creative photography. The experience had opened her eyes to so many things and provided professional growth.

"You were pretty stubborn about coming along," Brody reminded her.

She smiled at the memory. Her heart had leapt at his invitation, but her brain had immediately squashed it.

Turning around to face Brody, she pulled his coat and stood on her tiptoes to kiss him.

"Let's go inside. I have something for you," she said.

He followed her into the tour bus and they headed for his bedroom. Leaning up against the headboard was a gift wrapped in bright green paper and a big silver bow.

"What is this, Morgan?" he asked, looking confused.

"Well go on. Open it."

Brody leaned over the bed and picked up the present. After tearing off the paper, he held the gift with both hands, examining it closely. A lump built in his throat as he eyed the framed photograph of the shimmering ocean with the sunset hovering.

Offset in the corner of the photograph was Brody's house up on the cliffs in Santa Cruz, and there he stood looking out the window.

"Morgan ..." he said, touched.

She grabbed Brody's hand and looked into his eyes.

"You were meant to see me that day, Brody. I believe it without a doubt. I love you," she said.

Brody's hand trailed across the picture as he remembered the day Morgan fell and twisted her ankle. A smile surfaced and he chuckled.

"I saw you prancing around like ... like you were happy and free. I couldn't take my eyes off of you. I thought, 'What is she so happy about?' You were hypnotizing in a sense. I felt a pull to go down there and join you. Then you fell. So crazy. I didn't hesitate, just had to go help you. And ... it changed my life. I love you too, Morgan."

"We need a group hug, you guys. I love you so damn much, too," Jaxon said, nearly sobbing by Brody's bedroom door.

"Jaxon! I'm going to kick your ass." Brody chased him out of the bedroom.

All Morgan could hear were feet shuffling, followed by a thumping ruckus. She smiled and shook her head. Her mind trailed off.

Some things never change and there are times we wouldn't want it any other way. Change can also open doors ... push us off fences and force us to embrace the next challenge ahead. Tackling fear and stepping out of the comfort zone feels pretty damn good. Finding love ... even better.

Special thanks to Michele McFadden, preliminary editor.
Larry Kantor, photographer. CeAnn Velde Myers and
Dr. Paul and Julie Pflueger.

Made in the USA
Las Vegas, NV
18 November 2021

34774259R00099